Hi, I'm JIMMY!

Like me, you probably noticed the world is run by adults.

But ask yourself: Who would do the best job

of making books that *kids* will love?

Yeah. **Kids!**

So that's how the idea of JIMMY books came to life.

We want every JIMMY book to be so good

that when you're finished, you'll say,

"PLEASE GIVE ME ANOTHER BOOK!"

Give this one a try and see if you agree.

(If not, you're probably an adult!)

JIMMY PATTERSON BOOKS
for Young Readers

James Patterson Presents
Sci-Fi Junior High by John Martin and Scott Seegert
Sci-Fi Junior High: Crash Landing by John Martin and Scott Seegert
How to Be a Supervillain by Michael Fry

The Middle School Series by James Patterson
Middle School: The Worst Years of My Life
Middle School: Get Me Out of Here!
Middle School: Big Fat Liar
Middle School: How I Survived Bullies, Broccoli, and Snake Hill
Middle School: Ultimate Showdown
Middle School: Save Rafe!
Middle School: Just My Rotten Luck
Middle School: Dog's Best Friend
Middle School: Escape to Australia
Middle School: From Hero to Zero

The I Funny Series by James Patterson
I Funny
I Even Funnier
I Totally Funniest
I Funny TV
I Funny: School of Laughs

The Treasure Hunters Series by James Patterson
Treasure Hunters
Treasure Hunters: Danger Down the Nile
Treasure Hunters: Secret of the Forbidden City
Treasure Hunters: Peril at the Top of the World
Treasure Hunters: Quest for the City of Gold

The House of Robots Series by James Patterson
House of Robots
House of Robots: Robots Go Wild!
House of Robots: Robot Revolution

The Daniel X Series by James Patterson
The Dangerous Days of Daniel X
Daniel X: Watch the Skies
Daniel X: Demons and Druids
Daniel X: Game Over
Daniel X: Armageddon
Daniel X: Lights Out

Other Illustrated Novels and Stories
Laugh Out Loud
Pottymouth and Stoopid
Jacky Ha-Ha
Jacky Ha-Ha: My Life Is a Joke
Public School Superhero
Word of Mouse
Give Please a Chance
Give Thank You a Try
Big Words for Little Geniuses
The Candies Save Christmas

For exclusives, trailers, and other information, visit jamespatterson.com

JAMES PATTERSON

AND CHRIS GRABENSTEIN

ILLUSTRATED BY LAURA PARK

JIMMY PATTERSON BOOKS
LITTLE, BROWN AND COMPANY
NEW YORK • BOSTON • LONDON

The characters and events in this book are fictitious. Any similarity to real persons, living or dead, is coincidental and not intended by the author.

JIMMY Patterson Books / Little, Brown and Company
Hachette Book Group
1290 Avenue of the Americas, New York, NY 10104
jamespatterson.com

First paperback edition: December 2017
Originally published in hardcover by JIMMY Patterson Books / Little, Brown and Company, December 2013

JIMMY Patterson Books is an imprint of Little, Brown and Company, a division of Hachette Book Group, Inc. The Little, Brown name and logo are trademarks of Hachette Book Group, Inc. The JIMMY Patterson Books® name and logo are trademarks of JBP Business, LLC.

Middle School® is a trademark of JBP Business, LLC.

The publisher is not responsible for websites (or their content) that are not owned by the publisher.

The Hachette Speakers Bureau provides a wide range of authors for speaking events. To find out more, go to hachettespeakersbureau.com or call (866) 376-6591.

Library of Congress Cataloging-in-Publication Data
Patterson, James,
I even funnier : a middle school story / by James Patterson and Chris Grabenstein ; illustrated by Laura Park. — First edition.
pages cm. — (I funny)
Summary: "While on a mission to win the Planet's Funniest Kid Comic regional competition, New York middle schooler Jamie Grimm copes with rival comics and bullies, a buddy in trouble, and a sudden family emergency, all with a sense of humor and a loyal group of friends"—Provided by publisher.
ISBN 978-0-316-20697-6 (hardcover) — ISBN 978-0-316-24264-6 (international) — ISBN 978-0-316-20696-9 (electronic book) — ISBN 978-0-316-20695-2 (paperback) [1. Comedians—Fiction. 2. Contests—Fiction. 3. People with disabilities—Fiction. 4. Bullying—Fiction. 5. Middle schools—Fiction. 6. Schools—Fiction. 7. Long Beach (N.Y.)—Fiction. 8. Humorous stories.]
I. Grabenstein, Chris. II. Park, Laura, illustrator. III. Title.
PZ7.P27653Iae 2013
[Fic]—dc23
2013004379

10 9 8 7 6 5 4 3 2

LSC-C

Printed in the United States of America

For Jack, our house comedian.
—J. P.

For J. J. She funny, too.
—C. G.

PART ONE
Heard Any
Good Jokes Lately?

Chapter 1

IT'S FUN BEING FUNNY

Hi! I'm Jamie Grimm, and it's really great to be back in front of an audience again.

A little while back, I won a couple of contests and was crowned the Funniest Kid Comic in all of New York. Not just New York City, but the whole state!

Now I have a shot at being the Planet's Funniest Kid Comic.

"The planet Earth?" asks Phineas of—you guessed it—*Phineas and Ferb*. "Or Mars? We built a portal to Mars for the science fair once."

"Fun never falls too far from the tree house," adds Ferb.

Yep! Phineas and Ferb, the two hysterical stars from the Disney Channel, are now my close personal friends. They even go to school with me.

Nice try, kid. Only V.I.P.s and J.G.B.F.F.s allowed.
Who are those dorks with Jeter?
Thanks for the autograph, Jamie!
You okay?
Is that Phineas and Ferb, or do I need to stop eating my cereal with fruit punch?
J.G.
J.G.
NY
SECUR
BOSTON
NY

JAMIE FUNNIE
GRIMM MAKES ME GRIN!
HE FUNNY
SECURITY
Sorry, you're not on the list.
I swear I'm like Davey Grimm's best friend!
Me too!
You can keep your sign or your teeth.
JAMIE FUNNIE
We are never, ever, ever getting back together... because I met Jamie!
Make sure you get Jamie in the shot!
JAMIE FUNNIE

Derek Jeter, the shortstop from the New York Yankees, shows up at Long Beach Middle School because he wants *me* to autograph a baseball for *him*.

Taylor Swift comes to town to ask me to be the opening act at her upcoming concerts. "Jamie Grimm, I hear you're the Planet's Funniest Kid Comic!"

"Not exactly," I tell her. "First I have to win a regional competition in Boston. And then there are the semifinals in Las Vegas. And the final finals in Hollywood..."

"He's going to be a very busy boy," says Howie Mandel, one of the judges from *America's Got Talent.* He's come to Long Beach to help me train for the comedy competition. "Jamie needs new material. New jokes. A new hairdo. You like mine?"

Of course my best buds—Jimmy Pierce, Joey Gaynor, and Gilda Gold—are with me, too. We're on our way to school, where the principal has declared that today is Jamie Grimm Day.

"They're gonna give you your very own pep rally, dude," says Gaynor.

So after the cheerleaders do a "Jay-mee Grimm"

cheer, our school principal, Dr. Heinz Doofenshmirtz, or Doof as he likes to call himself, starts to make a little speech.

"Wait a second," says Phineas. "Your principal is *our* evil scientist?"

I shrug. "I guess he likes the cafeteria food."

Dr. Doofenshmirtz goes on with the quick speech. "Today, Jamie, we gather here to wish you luck as you prepare to take the second, third, and fourth steps toward your goal of being the Planet's Funniest Kid Comic! Break a leg, Jamie. Whoopsie!"

When Principal Doof says that, I know this has to be a dream.

Because, you know, all those steps he mentioned? I'd be happy just taking one.

Chapter 2

MEANWHILE, BACK IN REALITY…

Sometimes people in my dreams say crazy dumb stuff because they forget I'm in a wheelchair.

Hey, I don't blame 'em. I'd like to forget it, too.

But I can't.

Of course, I keep hoping that one day I'll see a commercial for a new wonder drug called something like Spinulax that will magically make me walk again. Unfortunately, it would probably come with a list of gross side effects like all those other pills they advertise on TV: *"Spinulax may cause constipation and diarrhea. Not to mention projectile vomiting. And sudden death syndrome—as in, oops, sorry, you're dead."*

When I wake up, I'm in my bedroom. In the

garage. Back in the real world. And I need to get my butt ready for school.

About my bedroom in the garage…when I moved to Long Beach to live with my aunt and uncle, the only spare room in the house wasn't actually *in* the house. This is why my clothes often smell like a Home Depot.

I call my aunt and uncle's house Smileyville because when I first got here, nobody ever smiled. Not even the dog, Ol' Smiler. He hadn't wagged his tail in so long his butt was brittle.

Anyway, I think I've finally figured out why the Smileys always look so glum.

It's the oat gruel.

That's what Mrs. Smiley serves for breakfast, *every morning*. You know how they say breakfast will stick with you? Well, her oat gruel sure will. It'll stick to your teeth and the roof of your mouth. *All day long.*

Quick, somebody call one of those cable TV networks! I have an awesome idea for a new reality show: *Breakfast With the Smileys!* It'll be the exact opposite of those shows about the Kardashians or the Real Housecats of Beverly Hills. No glitz. No glamour. No nothing.

"Have a nice day," says my aunt, Mrs. Smiley.

"Don't forget your lunch," my uncle, Mr. Smiley, reminds me.

"Be home by six," Aunt Smiley adds.

Yep. They're even blander than oat gruel.

But they took me into their home when I had no place else to go.

And for that, I will always be grateful.

No joke.

GUESS WHAT I SAW THIS MORNING?

As I'm heading up the sidewalk on my way to school, I see this really big, really green garbage truck grinding its way through something much worse than my aunt's oat gruel. We're talking mushy, juicy slop, slimier than the food scraps and sour milk sloshing around in the plate-scraper's barrel at my middle school's cafeteria.

And I start thinking about adding this to my comedy act....

If Long Beach wants a big green monster to gobble up its garbage, they should hire Godzilla. I hear they kicked the big guy out of Japan.

Something to do with him yanking the tops off too many Tokyo skyscrapers and munching on them like they were Nestlé Crunch bars. I think Godzilla ate a few subway sandwiches, too. The kind made out of *real* subway cars.

If Godzilla moved to Long Beach, he could stomp on down the streets, scooping up and emptying out Dumpsters. Even with his monstrous screeches, he'd be quieter than the guys who usually show up on our street at six AM to do drum solos on everybody's trash cans. Thanks to the garbagemen, nobody on our block needs an alarm clock.

Of course, if Godzilla did move to Long Beach, every time he went to, say, an all-you-can-eat buffet, a dozen waiters would probably disappear.

And you know what you'd find between Godzilla's toes?

Slow runners. (Sorry, I couldn't resist that one.)

When I meet up with Gilda Gold at the end of the block, I tell her my Godzilla the Garbageman idea.

She laughs and whips out her iPhone.

"That would make an awesome short," she says, starting to record. "We just shoot the garbage truck chewing up trash but dub in monster-movie music and really loud sound effects."

"And voices," I say. "Make 'em sound like they're coming from people buried underneath the garbage. *'Help meeeee!'*"

Gilda laughs.

I smile.

Gilda has a really cool laugh. A whole room can be cracking up, but you'll always hear her amazing giggle rippling through it all. It's the kind of laugh that makes a kid want to keep on telling jokes for the rest of his life just so he can keep hearing it.

Yep. Gilda's laugh is one of the reasons I want to be a stand-up comic more than anything in the world—even if I don't exactly fit the job description.

Chapter 4

WHERE I FOUND MY FUNNY BONE

Funny movies.

That's the first thing Gilda Gold and I ever talked about when my friends Gaynor and Pierce introduced us one day in the school cafeteria. Now she goes around Long Beach making short films. Maybe you've seen her latest video on YouTube—the one where two squirrels are watching a softball game while doing Abbott and Costello's classic comedy act "Who's on First?" I recorded the Costello lines, and Gilda did Abbott's. I'm not sure how she made the squirrels look like they were talking, but I think it had something to do with nut nibbling.

We had such a good time making that movie. Gilda and I both love funny flicks. Whatever Will

Ferrell, Ben Stiller, Jim Carrey, Chris Rock, and Kristin Wiig are up to at the multiplex. Also, any movie from Pixar. *Toy Story 3* is my favorite, but Gilda thinks *Wall-E* and *Ratatouille* are the best.

"Man, that is so gross," she says as the garbage truck dumps another load down its gullet. "What a great way to start the day."

I wiggle my eyebrows. "Yes, I've had a perfectly wonderful morning. *But this wasn't it.*"

Gilda laughs that laugh of hers. "That's Groucho Marx, right?"

"Yep. One of the funniest comedians ever. I've seen all the Marx Brothers movies. The Three Stooges, too."

When I was in the hospital, recovering from my accident, the doctors and nurses kept telling me "Laughter is the best medicine." (But let's face it: If you have a splitting headache, two aspirin might work better than a one-liner.)

They'd bring me all sorts of joke books and funny videos to help me feel better when I didn't think anything ever could. I read and watched everybody: the Marx Brothers, Lucille Ball, Woody Allen, Bill Cosby, Whoopi Goldberg, George Carlin, Jerry Seinfeld, Ellen DeGeneres, Robin Williams, Tina Fey, and more. I memorized entire jokelopedias.

I was recuperating for so long—doing rehab and physical therapy—I must've read, heard, or seen every joke cracked since the first caveman grunted "Knock knock" to one of his caveman buddies (and then conked the guy on the head with a club just so he could invent slapstick). And you know what? The doctors and nurses were right. All that laughing definitely helped me feel better. I almost forgot how miserable I was.

Almost.

You don't have to be stuck in the hospital to need a sense of humor, though. I mean, just going to middle school is a pretty scary thing for a lot of kids, because the *real* Godzillas hang out there.

Gilda and I are reminded of that as we head into Long Beach Middle School together. Gilda sees him first.

"Uh-oh," she says. "You know our perfectly wonderful morning?"

"Yeah?"

"It's about to get a whole lot worse than Dumpster diving with Godzilla...."

Chapter 5

BULLY FOR ME

Meet Stevie Kosgrov.

"Look at me, everybody," Stevie bellows into a microphone he probably stole out of the chorus room. "I'm a big, stupid comedian, just like Jamie Grimm!"

His mic doesn't have an amplifier. Stevie doesn't need one. The guy's a loudmouth.

"Well, if it isn't Nick the Hick," Stevie continues. "Nick's family's so poor, they eat cereal with a fork to save money on milk."

Ladies and gentlemen, no matter what he says, Stevie Kosgrov is *not* a comedian. He's a bully. Plain and simple. In fact, if it weren't for certain Third World dictators, Stevie would definitely be declared Bully of the Century. He once slugged a teddy bear that said the wrong thing when he pulled its string.

Stevie and his two buddies have turned the back corridor—the one everybody in my grade has to use to get to our lockers—into their private, insults-and-putdowns-only comedy club.

"There's a five-dollar cover charge," says Stevie's friend Zits.

"And a two-punch minimum," adds his other pal, Useless.

(Believe it or not, Stevie Kosgrov is an equal-opportunity bully. He gave Zits and Useless their nicknames. I find it pretty hard to feel bad for them, though.)

"Hey there, Jimari," says Stevie, zoning in on his next victim. "Calling you an idiot would be an insult to stupid people everywhere."

"Now pay up," says Zits, as Useless gives Jimari two knuckle punches in the arm.

"Let's go around the other way," whispers Gilda behind me.

"Nope," I say to Gilda. "My arms are too pooped." I move forward.

"Ladies and gentlemen, whaddya know—we have a surprise guest star," snarls Kosgrov. "Put your hands together for the Crip from Cornball."

Stevie's two pals snigger—just like they do every time he calls me that. See, I used to live upstate in a small New York town called Cornwall. Stevie, comic genius that he is, has turned Cornwall into Cornball. Clever, huh? The guy should write material for Jay Leno.

I inch my wheels forward again.

"What?" says Kosgrov. "You think you're the only

one who can be funny? No, wait. You're not funny. You're just *funny-looking*."

"Stevie," I say with a sigh like I'm bored. "I need to get to my locker. Can I ignore you some other time?"

"You think I'm gonna give you a free pass because you're a gimp?"

"Look, Stevie," I say. "I'm not offended by anything you say. I'm just glad you're finally able to string words together into sentences."

Now Stevie steps forward.

"You know what your real handicap is, Grimm? Your mouth. It won't shut up when it should."

He might be right, but he's made me too mad to care. I give my wheels a good shove and zoom straight up the hallway.

Yep. I'm going to roll right over Kosgrov.

I've already learned the hard way never to let him roll over *me*.

Chapter 6

WHO YOU CALLING CHICKEN?

Jamie!" shouts Gilda. "Don't!"

I totally ignore her and tear up the hall like greased lightning. (How they grease lightning, I haven't a clue.)

I'm pumping my arms furiously.

By the way, thanks to many months of using my arms instead of my legs, I now have a pretty good set of guns. It's like this T-shirt I saw at the rehab hospital: "Legs not working. Everything else meets or exceeds manufacturer's specifications."

"Yo! Jamie!"

My friends Jimmy Pierce and Joey Gaynor are in the hall now, too.

"Go for it, dude!" shouts Gaynor.

"Force equals mass times acceleration!" adds Pierce.

Have I mentioned that Pierce is a brainiac? He's telling me to increase my speed to better mow Kosgrov down.

Stevie doesn't move, though. He just casually crosses his arms across his chest and smiles at me, daring me to come at him.

I have the advantage. I have wheels and that whole "force equals mass times acceleration" science theorem thing on my side.

But Kosgrov isn't chickening out.

"*Banzai!*" I shout, and not because I love little trees. I'm about to crash like a kamikaze pilot, headfirst, into Kosgrov's gut, which is a pretty big (and soft) target.

Still he doesn't budge.

At the very last second, I chicken out. I cut hard to the right, swerve sideways, and crash into a wall of hardened steel lockers. I'm about to tip over and end up on my back like a cockroach (minus the kicking legs, of course), when Gaynor and Pierce rush in to catch me.

"Thanks, guys," I say as they prop me back up.

Then someone yanks the arms of my chair and spins me around.

Kosgrov.

"You always were a wuss, Grimm. Lucky for you, I'm too hungry to pound you for that little stunt. Now gimme your lunch money. Ever since you came to town, I don't get as much breakfast as I used to." He leans over me, giving me a full view of the food that got stuck in his teeth this morning.

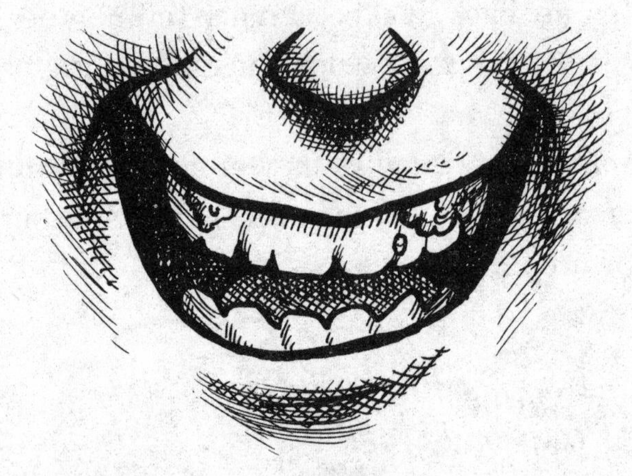

Did you notice the oat gruel?

That's right.

Stevie Kosgrov isn't just a bully. He's also Mr. and Mrs. Smiley's son.

Which makes him my cousin.

Which means he lives in Smileyville, too.

Stevie Kosgrov is like my own personal convenience store of pain and misery.

He gets to torment me 24/7.

Chapter 7

IT'S A GREAT DAY— FOR ABOUT TWO MINUTES

Right after science class—where I learn about the conversion of momentum between objects in collisions (or why my knees dented those metal lockers)—the school day suddenly gets great.

Cool Girl is in the hallway.

I call her Cool Girl because she's extremely cool and, as you can see from the helpful illustration, she's also a girl. Her real name is Suzie Orolvsky. Which is very hard to pronounce. I sometimes think her ancestors should've come to America with a few more vowels.

Anyway, Cool Girl is different from any other girl I've ever met.

For one thing, we've actually kissed. It was 8:43 PM. On the Long Beach boardwalk. A balmy seventy-six degrees. Stars were twinkling overhead. Two seagulls and a hermit crab were witnesses.

Hey—you never forget the details of your first kiss.

Another reason Cool Girl is different? She says

whatever is on her mind, whenever it happens to be there. If it's in her brain, it's going to come out her mouth. When I'm with Cool Girl, I feel like I can talk about anything and everything.

"Hey," she says when she sees me.

"Hey."

"You psyched for the regional competition up in Boston?"

As the winner of New York State's Planet's Funniest Kid Comic Contest, I'm supposed to represent the Empire State in the next round of the nationwide competition, which is being held at Boston's top club: Nick's Comedy Stop.

I shrug like the regionals are no big deal. "Sort of."

Cool Girl arches a skeptical eyebrow. "Sort of?"

"Well, it's not for a month. I need to work up some new material and—"

All of a sudden this guy cruises up the hall.

He looks like he just stepped out of an Abercrombie & Fitch catalog, except he's wearing clothes. He walks like a male model. You know—sort of sideways, with one hand in a pocket. Strut, swish, strut.

With the other hand, he's carrying a very heavy stack of books.

Cool Girl's books.

The ones I used to carry for her. (Well, she'd dump 'em in my lap and I'd roll along after her. I was like her personal library cart.)

"Hey, Suzie," says the buff dude.

Great. He *sounds* like those breathy guys in the perfume commercials. The hunks who ride the white horses and flick their incredible blond hair all the time.

"Hey, Ethan."

Double great. He's got a movie star name.

"Jamie?" says Cool Girl. "Have you met my boyfriend?"

Boyfriend?!?! Cool Girl has a Cool *Guy*?!?!

Remember how I said I really like the way she just blurts stuff out without thinking about what she's about to blurt? I'd like to take that back now, please.

"Ethan just moved here like a week ago from Malibu."

I swallow hard.

"California?" I squeak. At least Cool Girl can't hear my heart shattering like a souvenir Shrek glass from McDonald's when it hits the bathroom floor.

"Fer shure," says Cool Guy. "And you must be Jamie Grimm, the motor-skills-challenged comedian I've heard so much about."

Yeah.

That's me. The Motor-Skills-Challenged Motormouth.

Or, my new nickname, Fool Guy.

As in, I was a fool to think Cool Girl could ever really like me.

Chapter 8

A BURGER AND FRIES FIXES EVERYTHING

Before the final bell even stops ringing, I'm already out of school and up the boardwalk at my uncle Frankie's diner.

Yes. I am that fast. (It helps that it's mostly downhill.)

In case you couldn't tell by the menu, my uncle Frankie used to be the yo-yo champion of Brooklyn, a borough famous for people who shout "Yo!" and "Yo!" at each other. These days, he "rocks the baby" with one hand and flips burgers with the other.

His restaurant, Frankie's Good Eats by the Sea, is one of the oldest diners in all of the tristate area. That might be why the jukebox is filled with nothing but doo-wop classics from the 1950s and '60s.

I love the diner, but I love Uncle Frankie even more.

He's the one who first encouraged me to enter the Planet's Funniest Kid Comic Contest, because I'd entertain his customers by telling jokes when I helped out behind the cash register.

Now, whenever I have time, I roll behind the counter and start ringing (and cracking) people up. It's good practice—especially with those regionals in Boston breathing down my neck.

One customer loves anything by George Carlin, so I always have a pile of his brain droppings (that's what Carlin called one of his books) on hand.

"If the Cincinnati Reds were really the first major-league baseball team, who did they play?"

The customer busts a gut, so I give him one of Carlin's hippie dippie weather reports.

"The forecast for tonight is dark. Continued dark overnight, with widely scattered light by morning."

The next customer up to the register is another regular, Mr. Burdzecki. He's Russian and always wears a Cossack hat, even when the weather forecast is "hot" instead of "dark." He loves jokes by Russian comics, but the only Russian funnyman I know is Yakov Smirnoff, who mostly performs at his own theater in Branson, Missouri, these days. Lucky for me, Mr. Burdzecki doesn't mind a repeat every once in a while.

"You know," I say, "many people are surprised to hear that there are comedians in Russia, but they are there. They're dead, but they're there."

Mr. Burdzecki laughs like a big ol' happy bear. "You still funny!"

"Well, you're still a great audience."

"No." He slams his beefy fist on the counter. Coffee cups rattle in their saucers. "You funny. Even funnier than before."

"Okay," I say. "I funnier."

"Da."

"Jamie?" Uncle Frankie comes out of the kitchen twirling his yo-yo.

"Hey, Uncle Frankie. What's up?"

"Boston. The regionals. You working on your jokes?"

"A little."

He makes a "gimme, gimme" gesture with his free hand.

"Um, okay. A woman gets on a bus with her baby. The bus driver says, 'Ugh, that's the ugliest baby I've ever seen!' The woman walks to the rear of the bus and sits down, fuming. She says to a man next to her, 'The driver just insulted me!' The man says,

'You go up there and tell him off. Go on, I'll hold your monkey for you.'"

Uncle Frankie nods and fishes a scorecard out from under the counter. He flashes it at me.

"Come on. Hit me again."

"Okay," I say, thinking I'm on a roll. "I went to buy some camouflage pants the other day, but I couldn't find any."

Uncle Frankie groans. Winces a little. He holds up another scorecard.

He turns to one of the counter workers.

"J.J.? Take over the register. Me and Jamie need to hit the kitchen. We have some serious funny business to attend to."

Chapter 9

IF YOU CAN'T STAND THE HEAT...

Once we're in the kitchen, Uncle Frankie starts working me like he's a drill sergeant. Or a football coach. Maybe a child psychologist.

Actually, he's a little bit of all three, with a pinch of street-corner preacher and Jedi Master tossed in for good measure. He's pushing me to make my dreams of being crowned the Planet's Funniest Kid Comic come true.

"Remember, Jamie, no dream comes true unless you wake up and go to work."

I nod. "That's great advice, Uncle Frankie. Thanks."

Uncle Frankie smiles and twirls his yo-yo. "Well, I can't take full credit for that pithy little ditty. Anonymous said it first."

MAKE ME LAUGH, SOLDIER!
Drop and give me 20 jokes!
So, tell me. How did that joke make you FEEL?

"That Anonymous. What a busy guy. He must've written a new saying every day."

"So, have *you* written any new material for Boston?"

"A couple of things."

"Hit me with your best shot," says Frankie, taking a seat on a pickle bucket.

I launch into my rendition of what the Internet tells me is one of the funniest jokes in the world. It's based on a *Goon Show* sketch by the late, great Spike Milligan (yes, they had his old records in the rehab hospital library, too):

"Two hunters are out in the woods when one of them collapses. He doesn't seem to be breathing and his eyes are glazed over. The other hunter whips out his cell phone and calls 9-1-1. 'My friend is dead!' he gasps. 'What should I do?' The operator says, 'Calm down. I can help. First, let's make sure he's dead.' There's a silence. Then a gunshot. Back on the phone, the guy says, 'Okay, now what?'"

Uncle Frankie laughs.

Politely.

I was, you know, hoping for a little bit more. Like a guffaw, maybe even a chortle or a whoop.

"So, Jamie, tell me something. You ever been hunting?"

"No. Except once when I was like six."

"You went on a hunt when you were six?"

"Yeah. For Easter eggs."

Now, for whatever reason, Uncle Frankie cracks up. "Okay. More like that. Be you. Make it your own. I tell you, kiddo, your jokes are always a lot funnier when they come from who you are and what you've seen."

"Just stuff from my life?"

"That's right. The more real, the better."

I think about that for a second.

"Okay. Well, lately, I've realized I'm living my life like the guy who wrote that book *Under the Bleachers*."

"Really?" says Frankie, totally hooked. "Who's he?"

"I. Seymour Butts."

Uncle Frankie chuckles. So I keep going.

"I mean, look at me. I'm sitting here all day, living my life at belt-buckle-and-belly-button level. Unless I'm waiting in line. Then I'm staring at a sea of butts."

I shrug. "Seriously. Wherever I go, I have fannies in my face. And you can imagine my delight when it's Beanie Weenie day at the school cafeteria. There I am, cruising along, wishing my wheelchair was equipped with an optional gas mask..."

Uncle Frankie loses his yo-yo because he's laughing so hard he has to hold his sides. I think he might roll off his pickle perch.

"Okay, okay. Enough! That's the stuff. Give me

a dozen more bits like that, and I guarantee you'll cream 'em in Boston, kiddo!"

Wow.

I feel absolutely great. Uncle Frankie will do that to you.

Now the only thing I have to worry about is Nick's Comedy Stop serving those Boston baked beans I've heard so much about.

Chapter 10

LIFE IS FUNNY—AT LEAST, MINE IS

Coming home from the diner, I'm totally pumped about the upcoming competition.

Uncle Frankie is right. I'll just take stuff from my real life and turn it into comic bits.

For instance, Godzilla the Garbageman.

Or a school bully who calls himself an insult comedian.

I could talk about that tiny pink pill called Spinulax and then switch to my fast-talking announcer voice: "*Those actually breathing should not take Spinulax without first consulting a physician or a priest or an undertaker. Stop taking Spinulax if you develop bunny ears or moose antlers."*

Or how when some people see that I'm "handicapped"—a word that makes me feel like I should either be a horse or be playing golf—they start talking LOUDER.

Do these people think that after the car wreck, my ears ended up in my butt? That I'm sitting on 'em?

Then there's Cool Guy. The middle school male model. What's up with all those good-looking dudes like him in clothing catalogs? How come they're always pouting and looking bored? If I looked that good and had girls swooning over me, I'd smile. A lot.

And then, of course, there's school. What a concept. Think about it. It's an extremely strange way to spend the day—unless, of course, you grew up in a prison.

HOMEWORK
HOW TO MAKE WORDS HURT WORSE THAN FISTS
If Bob breaks six rocks in the hot sun and Jim breaks four, whose nose is getting broken while making license plates?
TODAY'S LUNCH
FRESH MEAT plus choice of milk
Line up! Today you will be assigned your bully. The two of you will share classes until you are paroled— err...graduate.
NO ·RUNNING ·SMILING ·CHANCE OF ESCAPE
MATH
ENG
MATH

When you're older, if you don't like people or they don't like you, you can just avoid each other. Adults have cubicles, gated communities, and country clubs, and they can screen their calls. If someone gives you a wedgie or a swirly at the office, you can call security. You can have the cops charge them with assault.

But kids my age? We *have* to go to school and spend all day, every day with bullies who want to insult us or stuff us into lockers or both. And if we don't show up, *that's* when the cops get called.

Uncle Frankie is so right. Forget all those joke books. My life is giving me all the material I need.

I'm all set to go into the garage and start writing this stuff down when Aunt Smiley calls to me from the front porch.

"Jamie? Can you come into the kitchen for a minute? Your uncle and I need to ask you a huge favor."

"Sure—" I start to say, until I notice Stevie Kosgrov standing behind her, shaking his head and giving me the stink eye.

Uh-oh.

Why do I think my life is about to hand me some new material?

Chapter 11

DIAGRAMMING MY DEATH SENTENCE

The very funny comedian Mel Brooks once said, "Tragedy is when I cut my finger. Comedy is when *you* fall into an open sewer."

Get ready to laugh.

Here comes my next open sewer.

"Like I said, Jamie," says Mrs. Smiley, "this is a *huge* favor."

"We need you to tutor Stephen," says Mr. Smiley.

"He's not doing very well in math or social studies," says Mr. Smiley. "Or that other one. You know. The one with all the scientific stuff. Science."

"He's flunking ELA and health, too," adds Mrs. Smiley. "But, well, we have to choose our battles."

"Will you help Stephen, Jamie?" says Mrs. Smiley. "You're doing so well in school."

That's because I do a few things Stevie never does, such as read, go to class, and study.

"You know, when I was Stephen's age," she continues, "I was struggling in school, and your mother—my big sister—well, she tutored me."

Great. Mrs. Smiley just went in for the kill. She mentioned my mom.

"Okay," I say. "I'll do it."

"Great!" says Mr. Smiley, practically leaping up from the table.

"We'll leave you two alone," says Mrs. Smiley with what amounts to a grin here in Smileyville. "So you boys can hit the books!"

Oh, boy. I really wished she hadn't mentioned hitting!

LION PIT
CAUTION: QUICK-SAND
LIVE SNAKES
CAUTION: LIVE SNAKES

Chapter 12

A LEGEND IN HIS OWN MIND

I have never been so happy to go to school.

Being there means I don't have to try to teach Stevie Kosgrov anything. For nearly eight hours, trained professionals are paid to take over for me.

I wish them luck.

Meanwhile, life decides to toss me another curveball.

My friends and I meet someone very, shall we say, *interesting* during our lunch period. Actually, *meet* isn't the right word. We're invaded.

The kid's name is Vincent O'Neil. He always thought he was pretty funny, but he didn't start messing with me until I won the Long Island's Funniest Kid Comic Contest.

Vince squeezes in between Gaynor and Pierce so he can tell us all how he's "one hundred thousand times funnier" than I'll ever be.

"I was going to enter that comedy contest you won," he says, "but something came up. I think it was my lunch. Hey, speaking of lunch, did you hear about the kid who drank eight Cokes? He burped seven up! Get it? SevenUp?"

"Got it," I say. "Thanks."

"Hey, why do seagulls fly over the ocean?"

Gilda sighs. "Why?"

"Because if they flew over the bay, they'd be bay-gulls. Get it? Bagels?"

"Yeah. Got that one, too," says Gilda. "Thanks."

"No problem. We aim to please. So you aim, too, please. I saw that once on a sign. Over a urinal!"

"Oh-kay," says Pierce. "Well, we only have another fifteen minutes to finish our lunch and—"

"Hey, what do Eskimos get from sitting on icebergs too long?"

Nobody says anything.

Except, of course, Vincent O'Neil. "Polaroids! Get it? Like hemorrhoids but I worked *polar* into it. Oh, what about this? Do you know why the Pilgrim's pants kept falling down?"

My turn to sigh. "Because he wore his belt buckle on his hat."

"Okay. You knew that one. Fine. Even a broken clock is right twice a day. Y'know, talking about Pilgrims reminds me of Thanksgiving, turkey, and *the turkey trots*. Did you know that diarrhea is hereditary? It runs in your jeans."

And with that, we all push back from the table. None of us are very interested in finishing our food, especially me, the guy who went with the sloppy joes.

Unfortunately, this is something that can happen after you win a couple of comedy competitions.

Somebody comes along who wants to knock you back down to earth.

And I say, let him try!

HYSTERICAL HISTORY

Bumping into Vincent O'Neil makes me think about what Uncle Frankie said. I need new material for Boston, not Vincent's stale and stinky fart jokes from *The Big Book of Butt Bugles and Blampfs*. So I keep my eyes open for new concepts to work out as I go to history class that afternoon.

We're supposed to give a presentation on our favorite president. I chose Millard Fillmore.

Why? Because nobody else will. Plus, his name is funny. Who knows? Maybe I'll get a whole bit out of him for Boston.

I roll to the front of the class and prop a portrait of President Fillmore on the flip-chart easel.

"Millard Fillmore was the thirteenth president

of the United States. Born in January 1800, he was named after a duck. No, I'm sorry. That was his brother *Mallard* Fillmore. *Millard* Fillmore was the last member of the Whig Party to ever hold the office of president. Probably because they all wore wigs."

Fortunately, our teacher, Mr. Johnson, is cracking up. Quick note for all you would-be class clowns: Make sure your jokes are smart enough to tickle the teacher's funny bone, too.

"I mean, can you imagine a big political convention with everybody wearing wigs like Lady Gaga? Fillmore started out as Zachary Taylor's vice president but took over after Taylor died because he drank a ton of cold milk and ate too many cherries at a Fourth of July celebration. All those cherries and milk gave Taylor gas. Really, really bad gas. Oh, by the way, today's dessert in the cafeteria? Cherry pie. Served with lots and lots of milk."

The whole class (except, of course, Vincent O'Neil) is laughing. So is Mr. Johnson.

"Yeah. History is funny. For instance, Millard Fillmore stopped Napoleon the Third from taking over Hawaii and making it French. Seriously. Can you imagine that? All those Hawaiians running around in

hula skirts and little berets, draping leis made of goat cheese and garlic over tourists' necks? Thanks to Millard Fillmore, it never happened."

I pause, waiting for the chuckles to die down. Then I wrap it up.

"Who says thirteen is an unlucky number? I say America was lucky to have Millard Fillmore as its thirteenth president!"

Everybody, including the teacher, applauds.

Well, not Vincent O'Neil.

He stands up at his desk.

"Not bad, Grimm. But let me tell you guys about President George Washington. Did you know they had to bury him standing up because he could never lie?"

The room groans.

Vincent keeps going. "Then there's Abraham Lincoln. At my old school, the teacher asked if I knew his Gettysburg Address. 'Gettysburg?' I said. 'I thought he lived in Washington.'"

More groans. Even Mr. Johnson rolls his eyes.

I'm the only one smiling at Vincent and his bad puns. Believe it or not, he's actually *helping* me

with my mission to win the Planet's Funniest Kid Comic Contest . . . .

Now I know what jokes *NOT* to tell in Boston.

WEEPING WITH THE WEEDWACKER

It's night.

I'm all alone.

There's no one here to laugh at my jokes.

And my garage bedroom smells like wet concrete mixed with motor oil.

I'm not all weepy like one of those black-velvet portraits of a bawling clown with tears streaking down his cheeks, but yes, I am feeling a little blue.

I'm sitting here thinking about my mom and dad, and my little sister, Jenny. And how the only family I have right now are the glum relatives who keep me tucked away in the garage with all the other junk that has wheels. It's the snowblower, the lawn mower, and me.

Plus, I just spent several hours tutoring my psychotic cousin, whose favorite subject so far is history—specifically the Spanish Inquisition and Attila the Hun, who was famous for torturing his enemies by hooking up four horses to their limbs and shouting, "Giddyup!"

Okay. You're right. I've also got Uncle Frankie. And if I had my choice, I'd be living with him. But it wasn't my choice. It was the judge's.

I guess this is why they say you can choose your friends but you can't choose your family.

But wait a second. *What if you could?*

That's it. I'm opening up a fresh notebook and jotting this down.

I feel a comedy routine coming on!

What if there were a TV game show where you could "Choose! Your! Family!"

I'd go with, I don't know, the Trumps. Then at least my wheelchair would be solid gold. Too heavy to budge, but classy.

No. The Hiltons! They own hotels. Hotels have swimming pools. I can't kick, but I sure can float. Of course, that might mean that Paris Hilton would be my stepsister and she'd ask me stuff like: "Walmart? Do they like make walls there?" (Seriously. She really said that once. I kid you not.)

Wait. I've got it. The Mannings. Yes! Eli and Peyton Manning could be my brothers. How cool would that be?

I'd get to go to all their games and warm up with the team. It'd be a blast. Except that my warm-up would be stone cold.

But they wouldn't care. Afterward we'd all go out for pizza and burgers and ice cream and strategize for the next week's games. Or maybe we'd just talk about movies and girls and other normal "brother" stuff.

Because when you get right down to it, that's what's really eating me up tonight.

I have friends, and I've got Uncle Frankie. Heck, I've even got the Smileys. But I don't have the closeness of a real family anymore.

And no joke will ever make that hole go away completely.

Chapter 15

LIVE FROM NEW YORK— IT'S JAMIE AND FRIENDS!

That Saturday, the most amazing thing happens.

Seems Uncle Frankie entered some kind of lottery (not the one with the lady popping the Ping-Pong balls out of the tubes) and actually scored four tickets to—drumroll, please—*Saturday Night Live*!

"An old yo-yo teammate of mine works on the show. Now," Uncle Frankie says with a twirl of the yo-yo and a twinkle in his eye, "I need to find three people to go with me. Any ideas, Jamie?"

Faster than a land shark delivering a candygram (a classic Chevy Chase bit from the very first season of *SNL* back in 1975), I say, "Pierce, Gaynor, and *ME*!"

This is the biggest, coolest surprise ever! When I was in the hospital, I watched every single episode of the late-night comedy show—going back all the way to 1975.

Since I'm in my chair, we get tapped by the NBC staff at 30 Rock for "floor seats." We're herded onto an elevator and whisked up to Studio 8H on the ninth floor.

The show opens with a funny bit about Santa Claus wrestling the Easter Bunny, and a cast member shouting, "Live from New York, it's Saturday night!"

The special guest host is one of my all-time favorite comedians, Steven Wright! His opening monologue has everybody—not just me—rolling in the aisles.

"There was a power outage at a department store yesterday," he says in his deep, sleepy voice. "Twenty people were trapped on the escalators."

A little after midnight, three of the female cast members put on ridiculous green costumes and do a skit that makes me feel like I have a solid start on my material for Boston. It's called "The Real Godzillas of Tokyo" and totally reminds me of my Godzilla the Garbageman bit. Theirs is a spoof on

This is funnier than a yo-yo in a wind tunnel!
WIPEZILLA:
REEEE

The Real Housewives of New Jersey and all those other reality TV shows where rich women get into fights and throw drinking glasses at each other.

The scene starts with the three big green dinosaurs (you could see their faces, like when Eddie Murphy did Gumby) casually hanging out on top of these really cheesy cardboard skyscrapers.

But then one of the Godzilla Girls says, "Green makes your butt look big," to one of the others. All three launch into slow-motion attack mode, shrieking "Reeeeee!," Tyrannosaurus rex–style. The three Godzillas take out the Tokyo Skytree tower.

After the show, Uncle Frankie, Gaynor, Pierce, and I hang out with the crowd on Rockefeller Plaza and snag a few autographs from the cast members.

And even though it's almost one thirty in the morning, our night isn't over.

"Who's hungry?" says Uncle Frankie.

We all raise our hands.

"Good. Time to hit the umbrella club!"

Chapter 16

FRANKENFURTER

I was kind of hoping that the Umbrella Club was one of those trendy celebrity hangouts in the city, with hidden entrances that you need a secret password and a bodyguard to get into.

Close, but no banana.

Uncle Frankie leads the way along the sidewalk to a hot dog cart (with an umbrella, of course) that's doing brisk early-morning business with a hungry mob of Rockefeller Center tourists.

We each get a hot dog with the works: mustard, ketchup-soaked onions, and sauerkraut.

After everybody's chomped down two or three bites, I improvise a quick bit.

"So, do any of you guys know what hot dogs are really made of?"

SNOUTS + TAILS
OLD GUM
SHOES
OLD JACK-O'-LANTERNS
SODA BOTTLES + CANS
DOG-O-MATIC
Hmm...needs more snout.
Premium
DIRTY WATER
HOT DOGS

"Stray wiener dogs?" says Gaynor. "From like the pound?"

"Nah, that would be gross. But they do use bubble gum scraped off the sidewalk. If you reheat it, it gets sticky and helps glue all the meat together. Especially if you toss in some library paste, too. Of course, I use the term *meat* loosely. It's mostly mashed cow nostrils, pig ears, turkey butts, congealed cafeteria scrapings, and dehydrated water. They grind up the gunk in a cement mixer and pump the goop down a funnel into pink bicycle tire tubes."

"What about rat droppings?" asks Gaynor. "I heard that sometimes rats poop in the meat vat."

"That's what they call all-natural flavorings."

"Delicious," says Uncle Frankie. "I think I'll have another. How about you boys?"

"Definitely," I say, tucking my arms up near my chest and screeching "Reeeeee!" like those Godzillas from *SNL*. "Jamie hungry!"

We all go back for seconds.

Because really, who cares what's in a hot dog, except maybe our moms, or, in my case, Aunt Smiley?

Okay. Gilda Gold would care. So would Cool Girl. Maybe even Cool Guy.

But us regular guys? We think hot dogs are great anytime, anywhere, any way you want 'em topped.

Including extra rat droppings. You know—the green chunky stuff the umbrella cart man calls relish.

Chapter 17

THE THREE AMIGOS?

Okay. This is nerve-racking. Gaynor and Pierce may be my best friends, but there's something I'm not sure even we can get through together. And it's all Gilda Gold's fault. I'm getting the shakes just thinking about it.

Let me back up a little bit (something, by the way, that's much easier to do in a wheelchair than, say, a La-Z-Boy recliner).

It's Thursday. We're all in the cafeteria—me, Gilda, Gaynor, and Pierce. The four of us are trying our best to ignore Vincent O'Neil, who's dropped by our table just so he can remind me that I only have three weeks to prepare for the Planet's Funniest Kid Comic regionals up in Boston, and that he is

now "a million times funnier" than me.

I have to give O'Neil credit. The guy is totally oblivious—even when he's bombing. He's like that Energizer Bunny. Even if no one is laughing, he keeps going and going and going.

He points to Pierce's burger. "Hey, you know what they call a cow with no legs? Ground beef! Get it? Because without any legs, it's on the—"

"I got it, I got it."

Gaynor tries to hide inside his hoodie.

"Hey, Joey."

Too late.

"What color is a belch?"

"I don't know, and, dude—I don't really care."

"Burple! Get it? It's like purple, but since a belch is a burp—"

"I GOT IT!"

Gilda is smart. She whips out her iPhone and starts fiddling with an app. Her eyes are glued to the screen.

So Vincent turns to me. "Okay, Grimm-meister. What goes 'Ha, ha, ha, plop'? Wait. You wouldn't know because you've never heard it. It's the sound of somebody laughing their head off! Get it? 'Ha, ha, ha, plop'?"

"Yes, Vincent," Gaynor, Pierce, and I say in three-part harmony. *"WE GOT IT!"*

"Ooh," says O'Neil. "I hope it's not contagious. Later, gents. Need to entertain the troops at the next table."

"Is he gone?" asks Gilda, without looking up from her iPhone.

"Yep, he's annoying Brightman Kornegay III and that bunch," I say.

"My heart bleeds for them," says Pierce.

"My nose, too," adds Gaynor.

"Get this, you guys!" says Gilda, swiping her fingers across her iPhone's screen. *"My Boyfriend Is a Vampire and a Werewolf III* opens this weekend. Wanna go?"

"Sure," the three of us say in unison.

Gilda finally looks up. Smiles. "Great. It's a date!"

Okay, I've heard of a double date with two guys and two girls, but three guys going out with one girl? Who's gonna pay for the popcorn? Gaynor, Pierce, and I exchange nervous glances. Then they both nod in my general direction. I've been elected to speak for the team.

"Um, with whom?" I say.

"Huh?" says Gilda.

"You said, 'It's a date.' We were kind of curious about *with whom*."

"Oh," says Gilda. "All three of you. I'll meet you there at seven!"

Chapter 18

TWO'S COMPANY, FOUR'S MORE FUN

"Hey, Jamie, Joey, Jimmy!"

Gilda waves at us from the movie theater box office as the three of us arrive for our Friday-night date.

"You guys know I only date boys whose names start with *J* and end with an *ee* sound, right?" Gilda jokes.

We three J-ees laugh. Nervously.

We also inhale one another's colognes. Guess everybody raided his dad's or stepdad's medicine chest tonight. Pierce smells like a pine tree. Or hay. Something farm-ish. And I'm pretty sure Gaynor dipped himself into a vat of Axe Body Spray.

Me?

Well, Uncle Smiley doesn't have much in the way of what you might call cologne. So I splashed on a little something in the kitchen. Yes, I smell like vanilla extract. But hey, who doesn't like cookie dough?

"I did the math," says Pierce, our resident statistician. (He once told me there's an average of 178 sesame seeds on a Big Mac bun.) "If the three of us chip in to buy Gilda's ticket, then we each—"

"You guys don't have to buy me my ticket."

"Um, I think we do," I say. "Otherwise, it's not officially a date. In fact, Vincent O'Neil would probably call it a prune."

Gilda laughs. "Well, I'm paying for the popcorn and drinks—"

"Nope," says Gaynor. "It's all covered."

And then, as our eyes pop out of our heads, Gaynor pulls a wad of cash out of his pocket.

"My mom gave it to me," he explains. "She said I should treat everybody to everything tonight!"

"Wow," I say. "We need to swing by your house tomorrow and say thanks."

"Nah," says Gaynor. "She's, you know, busy tomorrow."

"Well, what about Sunday?" asks Pierce.

"Busy," Gaynor says. "All next week, too. She's totally jammed. You guys can write her a thank-you note or whatever. Come on. The movie starts in like five minutes."

And of course, by five minutes, Gaynor means fifteen, maybe twenty. Yes, the lights will dim in five, but then we get to watch behind-the-scenes shorts that are really commercials for TV shows, and then movie trailers, which are, well, commercials for movies. Going to the movies is a lot like staying home and watching TV, except at the movies you can also get your eyeballs fried from the glow blasting out of an annoying texter's smartphone.

Of course, movie theater food is way different from the food you'd eat at home. For one thing, it's always huge. You order a small drink and it's the size of a toilet bowl. The "jumbo" drink is so gigantic that sometimes you'll find baby seals floating along on the ice cubes. The popcorn comes in trash barrel–sized containers, and you can smother it in fifty gallons of butter-flavored topping shot straight out of a golden-grease spigot.

By the way, whenever something is called BLANK-flavored, chances are there is absolutely no BLANK in it.

Gaynor's mom treats us all to jumbo sodas; enormous, crinkly boxes of Junior Mints, Goobers, and Raisinets; cardboard containers of nachos smothered in coagulated orange gunk (it might be cheese from a radioactive cow); and tubs of butter-flavored popcorn.

Believe it or not, the triple date (or whatever you call this) actually works. Since I'm kind of stuck in the theater's only handicapped-seating slot, Gilda and the other two Js shift seats periodically so Gilda ends up sitting beside each one of us for an equal amount of time. Pierce worked it all out on a flowchart. Something to do with combinations and permutations.

Who knew math could be so helpful? I mean, besides math teachers.

Anyway, *My Boyfriend Is a Vampire and a Werewolf III* is, in this critic's opinion, better than *I* and *II*. For one thing, when there's a full moon, the guy attacks himself. For another, my three friends and I are having an extremely good time—screaming, laughing, stuffing our faces.

By the way, in case you're counting, that's three incredibly cool things in a row: *Saturday Night Live*, the late-night hot dog feast, and now an awesome movie.

Sounds to me like my good luck is about to end.

Chapter 19

COMING ATTRACTIONS I DON'T WANT TO ATTRACT

I was stupid to think that Stevie Kosgrov would leave me alone if he ever found out I was out on a date.

He and his thug friends—Zits and Useless—tromp up the auditorium aisle swinging flashlights back and forth like, all of a sudden, they're ushers. Zits is even rattling a tin canister filled with coins—the kind they sometimes use to raise money at the movies for the Jimmy Fund, a charity that's been fighting cancer since 1948.

I think these guys are collecting for the Stevie Fund. It's been fighting everything it can punch since the day Stevie Kosgrov was born. Legend has it that at his birth, when the doctor slapped him on the butt, Stevie slapped back.

"Give it up, people," cries Stevie, totally ignoring the No Talking During the Feature Presentation rule, not to mention the theater's No Being a Jerk regulations.

Zits rattles the money can.

Stevie starts his charity spiel. "Folks, both the vampire *and* the werewolf want you to dig deep and give us everything you've got. We'll take cash, coins, and shoes. That's right, *shoes*. Preferably Nike or Adidas if you've got 'em."

"Sit down!" someone shouts from the darkness.

"Who's gonna make me?" Stevie shouts back, swinging the beam of his flashlight around the darkened auditorium, looking for his heckler.

And he finds me instead.

"Well, what do you know? It's the Crip from Cornball and his nerdy little friends. These three guys are on a 'date' with Gilda Gold. The one girl blind, deaf, and dumb enough to go out with them."

He grabs my popcorn bucket. I've only scarfed down about a pound, so there are maybe three pounds left in the tub. Stevie dumps it all on my head. I have butter-flavored topping drizzling down my ears.

"See? I did my homework, gimpweed. I stole that move from my new hero, Attila the Hun, who used to dump vats of boiling oil on people. You got greasy popcorn instead."

Stevie. My star history student. I guess all my tutoring is finally paying off.

He turns to Gilda.

"What're you drinking, Brillo Head?"

"Pepsi."

"Are you sure?"

"Uh, yeah. See? It even says *Pepsi* right here on the side of the cup. That's probably helpful for people like you, Stephen."

Stevie grabs the cup out of her hand and chugs a gulp.

"Nope. This isn't Pepsi. It's that new drink—Splash! See?"

And he empties the cup in my lap. It "splashes" all over the front of my pants. There's a mound of ice cubes melting over my zipper.

"Uh-oh," cracks Stevie. "Looks like Jamie wet himself again."

Zits rattles the coin can. "Please give to the Buy Jamie a New Diaper Fund!"

"Yeah," adds Useless. "His future *Depends* on you!"

"And remember," says Stevie. "We don't take credit cards, but we do take shoes!"

You know those three cool things in a row I was just talking about?

This wipes them off the scoreboard completely.

We're back at bummers ten, good times zero.

Chapter 20

JUST WHEN YOU THOUGHT SCHOOL WAS SAFE...

Monday morning, Gilda, Gaynor, Pierce, and I all walk to school together.

Well, they walk. I pump rubber.

For the record, our traveling to school together does not constitute another triple date. None of us is eating mass quantities of junk food purchased at a concession stand.

"I thought the movie Friday night was fun," says Gilda. "Well, until Kosgrov showed up."

"At least he only ruined the mushy part," says Gaynor. "When the girl was doing that slow-motion montage, trying to decide if she liked the vampire or the werewolf better."

"Correct me if I'm wrong," says Pierce, "but weren't they the same guy?"

"That's why they call it *My Boyfriend Is a Vampire* and *a Werewolf*," says Gilda with a giggle.

"Oh," says Gaynor. "I didn't catch that."

"Anyway," I say, "we should really thank your mom for paying for everything."

"I already did," says Gaynor, kind of fast (especially for him). "She says we're welcome."

"Your mom is significantly higher on my scale of coolness than most moms," says Pierce. He kind of pauses for a second, like he's debating what to say next. Then he asks, "Have you heard from your dad lately?"

"Nah," Gaynor scoffs. "He's in Florida. Haven't seen that slacker since Christmas two years ago."

We all just kind of nod.

I guess almost everybody, at one time or another, wishes they could play *Choose Your Family!*

We enter the school, where the vice principal, Mr. Sour Patch (his real name is Mr. McCarthy, but we call him Sour Patch because he always looks like he has a packet of lemonade powder dissolving on his tongue), is standing with his hands on his hips, staring at us. He's sort of like the Grim

Reaper. You do *not* want to be on his to-do list.

"There you are," says Mr. Sour Patch, scowling hard at Gaynor. "You need to come with me, Mr. Gaynor."

Gaynor doesn't budge.

"Is something wrong, sir?" I pipe up.

"You bet there is, Mr. Grimm. Your friend here has been breaking into lockers and stealing everything that isn't bolted down. Step into my office, Mr. Gaynor. We need to call your mother."

"She can't come to school…not today…."

"Really? Well, why don't we give her a call and she can tell me all about it."

Gilda, Pierce, and I glance at each other.

Is this where Gaynor got the money for the movies? we're all thinking.

Because from the way Mr. Sour Patch hustles our friend into his office, it sure looks like Gaynor is guilty, guilty, guilty.

GUILTY!!
GUILTY!!
GUILTY!!

PART TWO
Stop Me If You've Heard This One Before

Chapter 21

HURRY UP AND WAIT

Pierce and I wait in the school office for Gaynor, who disappeared behind the vice principal's "Discipline Zone" door.

I'm starting to wonder if Gaynor will ever come out. It's like we're playing *World of Warcraft* and he had to go into a dungeon all alone. And Mr. McCarthy is that dragon, Deathwing the Destroyer.

Pierce and I aren't the only ones in the waiting area.

First of all, there's Mr. McCarthy's secretary. I think she used to be a warden at the state penitentiary. Before that, I believe she raised farm animals over her head and guessed their weight at the county fair. Right now she's busy giving Pierce and me the stink eye. We're guilty by association. If we know someone who's been summoned to the VP's office, we must need a little time under the spanking machine ourselves.

There are all sorts of colorful characters lined up in the seats outside Mr. McCarthy's door—a half dozen of Long Beach Middle School's best and brightest, waiting their turn to see Mr. Sour Patch. Face it—you have to be pretty hard-core to end up in the vice principal's waiting room before first period is even over.

What'd you do this time?
I tried to divide a number by zero.
GUILTY. GUILTY. GUILTY. GUIL
PAROLE PASS
PAROLE PASS
PAROLE PASS
PAROLE PASS
TRVANT
SHOULDN'T IT BE SPELLED FONETIC?
Supposably.
It's still not a word.

One guy has so many tats, it's like he's a walking, slightly wrinkled comic book. Then there's the boy with the bloody nose.

"I didn't get in a fight!" he cries. "I have an upper respiratory infection!"

The warden lady chuckles like she's heard that one a hundred times before.

I see a girl with earrings dangling off every part of her head. She looks like she got too close to an exploding Slinky.

"This is worse than the waiting room at the doctor's office," whispers Pierce.

And I start thinking about how much of life is spent sitting around, just waiting for bad stuff to happen.

When the teacher walks up and down the aisle handing back graded tests, you have to sit there and wait till she finally, a year later, gets to you.

Doctors and dentists have entire rooms devoted to *waiting*.

Before the dentist drills your teeth, you have to wait and listen to the *whiiiiiine* of him drilling other people's cavities. Not only that, you have to read whatever magazines are lying around, usually junk from three months ago full of scratch-and-sniff perfume ads. This is why I always leave the dentist's office smelling like mouthwash and somebody's mother.

Finally, Gaynor, head hanging low, face redder than a stop sign, emerges from Mr. McCarthy's office.

"Next?" the vice principal says to a goth girl in the chair closest to his Discipline Zone door.

As she shuffles into the interrogation room, Gaynor comes over to me and Pierce.

"Nice knowing you guys," he says. "It's been a real honor."

"What happened?" asks Pierce.

"There's going to be a disciplinary hearing."

"And then what?" I ask.

Gaynor shrugs. "I guess I'm going to be kicked out of school."

FREE JOEY!

After school, we have a last-gasp Free Joey strategy meeting at Frankie's Diner.

"What'd you tell your mother?" I ask.

"Nothing," says Gaynor. "At least not yet. We couldn't get hold of her on the phone."

"Won't she have to come to the hearing?" asks Pierce.

"I guess," says Gaynor. "She may not be able to."

Gilda's shocked to hear it. "Wha-hut?"

"She may not make it. She's still kind of busy."

"Too busy to help you *not* get suspended from school?" says Pierce, because we're all thinking it.

"Yes. She's that busy. Now can we please quit talking about my mother?"

There's a long, awkward silence. You could hear crickets if, you know, Uncle Frankie's restaurant had a bug problem.

"Well," I say, "maybe there's a way we can prove to Mr. Sour Patch that you didn't steal anything."

"Or," Gilda says excitedly, "we could stage a ginormous rally! Get some big-name rock bands and singers to hold a benefit concert for the Joey Gaynor Freedom Fund!"

Pierce, Gaynor, and I nod.

And then Gilda says, "So, um, do you guys know any rock stars?"

The three of us shake our heads.

"Nope."

"Not me."

"Oh-kay," says Gilda. "How about a bake sale?"

"No," says Pierce. "We need to hold a protest rally. We march around the school with signs and banners."

"Right," I say. I suddenly remember a famous quote from history class by some guy in the Revolutionary War. I hold up my hands like I'm carrying a giant sign. "Give Joey Liberty or Give Him Death!"

"Whoa," says Gaynor. "Can we skip the death part?"

"Um, sure. How about 'It's better to die fighting for freedom than to live life in chains!'"

"Again with the death?" says Gaynor.

"How about we go with what Abraham Lincoln once said," suggests Pierce, our walking Wikipedia. "'Those who deny freedom to others deserve it not for themselves!'"

"So," I say, "we kick Vice Principal McCarthy out of school, too?"

"How's that gonna work?" asks Gilda.

"Not very well," says Gaynor.

That's when Uncle Frankie comes over to our booth.

"Hey, Joey," he says. "I heard the bad news."

"Really?" I say, because I'm sort of shocked that what goes on in Long Beach Middle School doesn't stay in Long Beach Middle School.

"How'd you hear?" asks Gaynor.

Uncle Frankie shrugs. "I work in a diner. I hear everything. So, look—you need anything, you let me know."

"Do you know any good slogans?" asks Gilda. "For a banner we can hang up at school?"

Uncle Frankie twirls out his yo-yo and reels it back in a couple of times.

This is how he thinks deep thoughts.

"Yeah. Okay. Here's one we used all the time, especially before a big yo-yo tourney: 'Teamwork makes the dream work!' "

All four of us just nod.

"Oh-kay," I say. "Thanks, Uncle Frankie."

"My pleasure. And, Joey? Hang in there, kiddo, okay?"

"Yes, sir. I'll try."

When Uncle Frankie's gone, we all sip our sodas in silence, because we don't have a single decent idea about how to help Gaynor.

He is definitely dead meat.

Chapter 23

CALLING ALL GODS!

That night, after tutoring Stevie with multiplication-table flash cards his little brother let us borrow, I'm about to crawl into bed. But I decide to say a prayer first.

"Hi, God. It's me again. Jamie Grimm. Thanks for, you know, everything. That sunset tonight was awesome. One of your ten best. Love how you worked in all those golds and purples. Oh, and thank you for not letting my cousin Stevie kill me today, especially when he got stuck on his nine times tables.

"Anyway, I'm not really here tonight to pray for myself. If it's okay, I need to ask a favor for a friend, a great guy named Joey Gaynor. Don't let his tattoos or nose ring fool you. Joey has a good heart. Seriously. He was one of the few kids in Long Beach to be nice to me when I, you know, *rolled* into town. Now he's in big trouble. They say he's been stealing stuff at school. I don't think it's true, but, well, you might have some inside information on that, since you are omniscient and have videos of everything everybody down here does every day.

"But even if Joey did steal, well, I'm sure he feels terrible about it now. He'll give it all back, too. So please, God, don't let them kick him out of school. Maybe he made a mistake. You know what they say: 'To err is human, to forgive is divine.' And they don't get any more divine than you, sir, so I hope you'll cut Joey some slack. Like I said, he's a good kid. I swear on a stack of Bibles, a book I'm sure you're familiar with. It's a good read, sir. Action, adventure, life lessons. I don't mean to go all brownnoser on you here, but, well, whatever you can do for Joey, er, Joseph, will be greatly appreciated. Thanks for listening. Have a good night. If, you know, it's night where you are.

"Oh, and please take good care of my mom and dad and my little sister. Tell them I miss them. I miss them a lot."

★ ★ ★

Okay. Done. I tried, anyway.

I lock my chair at an angled position next to my bed, putting one fist at my hip and another at the edge of the mattress. I rock forward on my bed arm and use the hand by my hip to push my weight off the chair and transfer it onto the bed. Once I'm on, I put both hands behind my hips and get ready to slide myself up the covers.

But I stop.

Because I think Gaynor may need a few more prayers.

So I plead his case to Apollo, Hera, Poseidon,

Dionysus, and Artemis—Greek gods I read about in Rick Riordan's books.

And while I'm at it…

I toss up a few quick pleas to the top god from that movie *The Immortals* and ask Zeus to lend Gaynor his Warhammer of Ares, the thing Zeus used to smash the Titans' Epirus Bow to bits. I also have a quick chat with the Norse god Odin (you know, Anthony Hopkins) from that other movie *Thor*.

Hey, Gaynor needs all the help he can get.

I just hope God (or one of his backups) is listening.

Chapter 24

WISH THIS WAS A BASKETBALL COURT...

On the day of the big hearing, Gaynor, Pierce, and I go to school dressed like the Blues Brothers or those dudes from the *Matrix* movies, minus the sunglasses and the random philosophical ramblings.

Gilda would've joined us, but she doesn't own a dark suit.

We're trying to look respectable, like attorneys on TV do when they head to court.

(I mean the classy lawyers from shows like *Law & Order*, not the cheesy ones who do their own late-night TV commercials and say stuff like "Have you or a loved one slipped on a grape at the grocery store? Your case may be worth millions of dollars. We're the lawyers at I Can't Believe It's a Law Firm, and you'll pay us no fee unless we win your case, in which case you will pay us those millions of dollars I was just talking about.")

Vincent O'Neil sees us in the hallway and starts making cracks.

"Hey, guys. Nice suits. Who's about to die? Oh, right—Joey 'The Locker Looter' Gaynor."

"Very funny, Vincent," says Pierce. "Now, if you'll excuse us…"

"Why? Did you guys just fart?"

Gaynor just sort of glares. O'Neil scoots up the hall, laughing hysterically at his own joke.

"Mr. Gaynor?" The vice principal's secretary calls from the school office. "Is your mother here?"

Gaynor shakes his head. "No, ma'am."

The secretary gives that a *harrumph*.

"Mr. McCarthy is inside," she says. "Waiting."

Gaynor, Pierce, and I march solemnly into the office.

"Mr. Grimm? Mr. Pierce?" says the secretary. "What do you boys think you're doing?"

"Standing up for Joey," I say, even though technically it's impossible for me to stand up.

"Me too," says a voice behind us.

I wheel around. It's Uncle Frankie.

"Hiya, Clarice," he says to the secretary.

She blushes a little. "Francis."

"Need to have a quick word with John. It's about, you know, this Joey Gaynor situation here."

"I see."

"I know John's a busy man, but this will only take a minute or two."

"Very well, Francis. Wait here."

"Thanks, Clarice."

The secretary goes back into the office. We look at Uncle Frankie, puzzled.

He shrugs. "Back in the day, John McCarthy and I were on the same yo-yo team. Clarice, too. We took State that year."

Wow. I guess those multicultural mannequin munchkins at Disney World are right.

It *is* a small world after all.

One minute later, Uncle Frankie is in the vice

principal's office, chatting with his old friend.

Five minutes later, he's back in the hall.

"Okay, Joey. Me and John had a little chat. They're gonna cut you a deal. You'll be serving detention for a month, but you get to stay in school."

"For real?" says Gaynor with a catch in his throat.

"Yeah. We're gonna make a few other changes, too, but for now—go hit the books. I got bigger fish to fry. Literally. My fishmonger dropped off a hundred-pound cod this morning."

"Thanks, Uncle Frankie," I say.

"No problem. We gotta look out for each other. Am I right, boys?"

"Yes, sir!"

Gaynor, Pierce, and I head off to class, high-fiving as we race down the hall. Probably not our smartest move after Gaynor just escaped being expelled. I catch one more look at Uncle Frankie about to walk out the front door, and I shoot him a thumbs-up.

I guess God *was* listening after all.

And he knew exactly who to call.

MRS. GAYNOR'S EXCUSED ABSENCE

That afternoon, we learn the real reason why Mrs. Gaynor couldn't come to her son's hearing.

She's in the hospital.

Memorial Sloan-Kettering Cancer Center in New York City. She's getting her third round of chemotherapy.

This is why she was "too busy" to come to school in the morning.

It's also why Gaynor didn't want us dropping by his house to thank his mom for treating us to the movies. She probably wasn't there. Or, if she was, she might've been feeling pretty queasy from all her cancer treatments.

As I'm heading out of school, Uncle Frankie

pulls up in his van and tells me he's going to drive Gaynor into the city to see his mom.

"You knew about this all along?" I ask.

"No, kiddo. I only heard about it the other day. Some of Mrs. Gaynor's pals were at the counter, talking about how sad it was to see somebody so young get so sick."

"Oh. So that's what you meant when you told Joey how sorry you were about his bad news."

"Yeah."

"And then you told Mr. McCarthy what was going on?"

Uncle Frankie nods. "Your vice principal may look like a sourpuss, but he's really a cream puff. We can't have Joey living all by himself in an empty apartment while his mom's in the hospital. So if she gives her permission, Joey's gonna be staying with me for a while. I want you to move in, too, while he's there. It'll make things a lot easier for Joey. I've talked to your aunt about it already."

My eyes practically pop out of my skull. What a day. *All* my prayers are being answered! I just wish some of Gaynors's were, too.

"It'll only be a temporary situation," says Uncle Frankie. "But I figure the three of us can deal with this easier if we're all together. We can also get you ready for those regionals up in Boston. Joey can be your second."

"Huh?"

"You know, like in boxing. Joey will be your corner man. And like they say in the Miss America pageant, 'should you for any reason be unable to fulfill your duties,' maybe Joey could take your place onstage."

We both think about that for a minute.

"Bad idea?" says Uncle Frankie.

"Terrible."

We both start laughing, which makes me feel better, just like it always does.

I'm thinking I should go visit Mrs. Gaynor. Tell her a few jokes.

After all, laughter is the best medicine. And it won't make you sick to your stomach, like chemotherapy does—unless Vincent O'Neil is the one telling the jokes.

Chapter 26

TRUE CONFESSIONS

That night, as we're helping Uncle Frankie lock up the diner, Gaynor has a confession to make.

"Mr. Frankie, sir?"

"Yes, Joey?"

"I need to tell you something."

"I'm listening, my son." (I think Uncle Frankie's heard a priest say that to him a few times.)

"Well, you know that stuff about me stealing junk out of lockers?"

"Yes?"

"It's true. I did it."

"I know. Mr. McCarthy showed me the video from the school's surveillance cameras."

"It's how come I had the money to treat everybody to the movies."

"I see."

"I had my reasons for doing it, sir...."

"Go on."

"Well, my mom wasn't home. She was in the hospital. And my lame-o dad is down in Florida acting like he doesn't even have a son or a sick wife. I mean, uh, ex-wife. And we don't have any other family living here in Long Beach, and, well, I was hungry. I needed money for dinner."

"Just for the record, Joey, you ever get in that type of situation again, you can always eat here. For free. We'll work something out. Dishwashing or whatever."

"Thank you, sir. But, well, the McRib sandwich was back at McDonald's, and, well, you don't have a McRib on your menu...."

"Whoa. Hang on. You didn't need to steal so much loot for one lousy McRib. You didn't *have* to buy everybody's movie tickets the other night. Why'd you burglarize so many lockers?"

"I dunno. I guess I was mad. At my mom for getting sick. At *me* for not being able to do anything to help her. At the world for being so unfair. I mean, why did my mom have to be the one to get cancer?"

"I see. Why not someone else's mom?"

Gaynor thinks about what he just said. "I didn't mean it like that."

"I know."

"I guess I'm a pretty lousy kid, huh?"

"Nah, Joey," says Uncle Frankie, following us out of the diner and locking the door. "You're just a kid dealing with some pretty grown-up stuff. But always remember what Eleanor Roosevelt used to say."

"Who?"

(Gaynor's not really one for history. Maybe I can tutor him next.)

"She was FDR's wife," says Uncle Frankie.

"Oh. Cool. So who's FDR?"

"That's not important. Not now, anyway. What is important is a little bit of advice Mrs. Roosevelt passed out: 'A stumbling block to the pessimist is a stepping-stone to the optimist.' So we learn from this, we turn it into a stepping-stone, and we move forward."

"Okay. Thanks. But, uh, where are we going?"

"Right now, home. You two need to hit the hay. There's school tomorrow."

"Yeah," says Gaynor, sounding relieved. "Thanks for that."

"Thank me after you take that math test in first period."

"What?"

Frankie shrugs. "Hey, you missed math today. Mr. McCarthy gave me a heads-up. You also have ELA homework."

"Okay." Gaynor doesn't look happy about it, but my guess is he'll do his homework.

"So what's ELA?" Frankie asks.

"What they used to call English," I say.

"So why'd they change it to ELA?"

"Because...I guess it would be plain English to call it English. And if there's one thing we learn in ELA...it's how *not* to speak plain English."

Frankie chuckles, and even Gaynor smiles. Not knowing the answer to a question is always a great opportunity to make a joke.

Gaynor and I share the spare bedroom in Uncle Frankie's tiny apartment, which is in a five-story walk-up just down the block from the diner.

Fortunately for me, he lives on the first floor.

We're both pretty beat, so the room gets quiet really fast. You can't hear anything except the ocean crashing against the shore a block away. I'm drifting off to sleep when Gaynor whispers, "Thanks for everything, Jamie."

"Well," I say, "I didn't really do anything except have a cool uncle. I hope I turn out to be as good a guy as Frankie when I grow up."

"You're already a great friend."

"I'm not sure I'm all that *great*, but I *am* a friend with wheels. And don't you forget it."

Gaynor laughs. "I won't."

"Good. Because if you ever need me, I'll be there faster than anybody else."

RIDE 'EM, COWBOY!

Saturday morning—after we make our beds, clean our room, and watch a couple of cartoons (hey, it's research for my act)—Uncle Frankie announces it's time for Mustang Wrangling.

Gaynor and I have no idea what he's talking about. Maybe there's a rodeo in town. Maybe a pack of wild horses escaped from the Bronx Zoo and is stampeding across the Brooklyn Bridge toward Long Beach.

"We need to go to the diner, boys," Uncle Frankie explains. "It's time to broaden your horizons."

"You're gonna make us eat horse meat?" says Gaynor.

"No. I'm talking about, you know, guy stuff.

Learning how to handle a muscle car, like my classic 1967 Ford Mustang convertible!"

The three of us troop down the block to the diner, where Uncle Frankie's cherry-red ride sits in the parking lot, gleaming in the sun. A pair of fuzzy dice dangle from the rearview mirror. His vanity plates read STAAANG, which I'm guessing is slang for Mustang.

"Joey," says Uncle Frankie, "climb in the passenger seat."

"Cool!" Gaynor hops in.

"Okay, Jamie. You too."

"Uh, I'll wait till you take Joey for a ride. I don't think I can get into the backseat."

The convertible is kind of tiny. You have to fold down the front seats to climb into the back. I'm not so good at climbing.

"You're not sitting in the backseat, Jamie," says Uncle Frankie.

"Huh?"

"I want you behind the wheel, kiddo. After all, one day this car is going to be yours."

"What?"

"I'm gonna give you my Mustang."

"Why? I won't ever be able to drive it."

"Really? Why not?"

"Um, correct me if I'm wrong, Uncle Frankie, but don't drivers need to work—oh, I don't know—the gas and brake pedals? Don't you need to use your feet?"

"Not necessarily, kiddo. See, I've been talking to my friend Ralph. You know Ralph, right? From the garage over on East Market Street."

"Sure. The guy with the black fingernails who likes my Tim Allen jokes."

"That's the guy. And for the record, that black

gunk is grease, not nail polish. Anyway, me and Ralph, we've been talking. Turns out it's easy-peasy for him to install what they call hand controls. You operate the gas and the brakes with handles, which Ralph attaches to the steering column. They're like the handlebar gizmos on a bike or motorcycle."

"I don't need my legs?"

"Nope. You just need to haul yourself into the car, toss your chair in the backseat, and hit the highway."

Okay. This is kind of choking me up.

Unless you've spent some time in a wheelchair, you have no idea what Uncle Frankie is offering me. Freedom. Independence. Mobility.

With a car, I can hit the open road. I can go to any college I want, not just the ones near the city bus stops. I can go see things I'd started thinking I might never see.

I angle my chair up beside the driver's door and transfer myself into the driver's seat.

And I can imagine everything.

Buzzing down the highway in my STAAANG. The wind whipping through my hair. Cute girls waving at me from *their* convertibles as I whizz past. Bugs splattering against my teeth because I'm smiling so much.

"Yep. Sally's a mighty fine gal," says Uncle Frankie.

"Sally?" I say.

"That's her name. You can change it when the Mustang's yours—which she will be on your sixteenth birthday."

"No joke?"

"Nope. Jokes are your department."

Have I mentioned how much I love my uncle Frankie?

Yeah. I thought so. Because I really, really do.

Chapter 28

GETTING HOUSE-TRAINED

Early Sunday morning, Uncle Frankie takes Gaynor and me into the kitchen (at his apartment, not the diner) with a sack of groceries.

We've got eggs, milk, bacon, sausages, pancake mix, syrup, orange juice—everything to make a major-league breakfast.

And a mess.

"I thought we'd whip up some French toast," says Uncle Frankie.

"Should I plug in the toaster?" asks Gaynor.

"No, Joey. You should pay attention."

And Frankie shows us how to crack an egg—with one hand.

"So your other hand is always free to loop-the-

loop. See, if you know how to cook your own food, you'll be able to take care of yourselves, no matter what. Even if you're on your own."

I sometimes forget that Uncle Frankie used to be married.

I met his wife, Aunt Rose, a long time ago—back when I was like three and my mom and dad and I came to Long Beach for summer vacation. I remember she wasn't feeling very well that summer. We came back to Long Beach in early winter for Aunt Rose's funeral.

Uncle Frankie has been alone ever since.

Well, not entirely alone. He has a ton of friends at the diner. But that's not the same thing.

"Okay," says Uncle Frankie, "challah bread makes the best French toast. We dip it in this batter. Make sure you coat both sides. But don't let it get so soggy the bread starts falling apart. Then we pop it in a hot buttered skillet. Brown each side. Voilà."

Gaynor and I each take turns making our own French toast.

Then we sit down and smother it with maple syrup. Frankie has cooked up some omelets, pancakes, and bacon for us, too.

We all pig out.

When breakfast is done, Uncle Frankie dabs at his lips with a paper towel, which he tells us is what guys sometimes use for napkins when nobody's looking.

"But don't eat over the sink too much," he advises. "It's not classy."

Gaynor and I both nod. We're taking mental notes.

"And now, gentlemen, we learn the most important lesson of all. We learn how to clean up our own messes."

"Um, I've got homework," I say.

"Yeah," says Gaynor. "Me too."

"I know," says Uncle Frankie. "And this is it. Who wants to wash and who wants to dry?"

Chapter 29

HOW TO DO NOTHING, AND DO IT WELL

Sunday afternoon, Uncle Frankie comes into the living room with a stack of DVDs.

"Okay, guys, enough with the domestic engineering. We need to prep Jamie for Boston."

"You read my mind!" I say.

"These are some sitcoms I bought at a yard sale. I thought they might help. Like this *Seinfeld* show. What makes it so funny?"

And I have another "aha!" moment.

"The same thing you told me to do!" I say. "It pulls jokes from real life!"

Frankie and Gaynor sit down on the couch while

I slip the *Seinfeld* Season 3 disc into the DVD player.

"The creators of *Seinfeld* always said it was a show about nothing. But it's really a behind-the-scenes look at how to develop material for your stand-up act. And it's not about jokes. It's about everyday life. You know, what you'd consider nothing special at all, like making a mess cooking French toast. You take some of the ordinary stuff that happens and poke fun at it," I start.

Up comes the DVD menu. I pick one of my favorite episodes: "The Alternate Side."

"Okay, this is a bit from Seinfeld's act."

The show opens with Jerry Seinfeld holding a microphone in a bright white spotlight in front of a red curtain at a comedy club. He's doing a stand-up routine about car alarms.

"It seems to me," he says, "that the way they designed the car alarm is so the car will behave as if it was a nervous, hysterical person. Anyone goes near it, anyone disturbs it, it's *aaa-waa-waa-waa*." He starts waving his arms around like a lunatic.

"Funny," says Uncle Frankie.

COMEDY = TRAGEDY + TIME!
JOKE ABOUT WHAT YOU KNOW
REAL LIFE = REAL FUNNY!
REAL LIFE

"But watch!" I say. "See, this next scene is supposed to be from Jerry's real life."

Jerry and his friend George enter Jerry's apartment. Jerry can't believe that his car was just stolen.

"It was parked right outside," he says.

"Was the alarm on?" asks George.

"See?" I say, pushing the Pause button. "That's where he got the idea. Something bad happened in his life and he worked it into his act."

"Um, does that mean you're gonna talk about me again?" asks Gaynor. "Because I've been going through a whole bunch of bad stuff lately."

"I dunno. Maybe." I think about it for a second and get an idea. "I might mention that I have a friend at school who got caught stealing stuff out of lockers. Poor kid. He still doesn't know what to do with all those posters of the guys in One Direction."

Uncle Frankie laughs. "Bingo! That's the stuff, kiddo!"

"Do it, Jamie," says Gaynor. "And use my name! Please?"

When I won the New York State contest, I told a joke or two about Gaynor. A lot of girls at school thought that was cool and started going crazy all over him.

I think he's hoping for a repeat in Boston.

Chapter 30

A BATTLE OF WITS?

Back at school on Monday, I'm feeling pretty good.

Life keeps handing me new material. For instance, after thinking about Gaynor and the lockers, I decide to roll up and down the halls during class changes and check a few out. See what people really have plastered on their walls.

It's like some kids are building little houses inside their tiny metal storage units. This one girl, Ashleigh—I kid you not—has a polka-dot chandelier hanging off her coat hook, zebra-print wallpaper on the side walls, and a lime-green shag carpet on the floor. She'd probably put in a microwave and a TV, but her locker doesn't have electricity. Or cable.

I'm about to whip out my notepad when I sense somebody standing behind me.

"Hey, Jamie! Wocka-wocka!"

Vincent O'Neil is in the hall, making like Fozzie Bear from the Muppets.

"Quick question, Jamester: Why did the Cyclops close his school?"

So much for coming up with new material. It's time for jokes that are older than dirt on the moon.

"Because he only had one pupil," I say with a sigh.

"Oh, you heard that one before?"

"Yeah. See, a while back, I more or less memorized a bunch of joke books, but now…"

"So where did the pencil go on vacation?"

"Pennsylvania."

Vincent puts his hands on his hips. Wrinkles his nose at me. "Oh, you think you're so funny. Jumping on my punch lines."

"I'm not jumping on anything," I say. "The doctors tell me it's medically impossible."

"What? Was that supposed to be funny? Do you see me laughing? I am so not laughing."

"No, Vincent. I'm just saying that maybe you ought to—"

"Don't sit there giving me advice, Grimm. I'm Vincent O'Neil, and I am the *real deal*! I'm ten billion times funnier than you'll ever be."

"Maybe so, Vincent. Excuse me. I gotta—"

"After school."

"What?"

"You and me. Outside. We settle this once and for all."

I am so confused. "Settle what?"

"Who's the funniest kid at Long Beach Middle. This is a formal challenge to a duel that you cannot refuse unless you want me to tell everybody you're too big a chicken to stand up for yourself!"

I grin. Vincent came pretty close to a decent joke there.

"So how's this competition work?" I ask.

"We take turns telling jokes. The comic who gets the most laughs from the crowd wins."

We're already drawing quite a crowd in the hallway.

I can't back down. If I do, everybody at school will think I won the New York State contest because the judges took pity on me, a poor little crippled kid in a wheelchair. Besides, maybe if I beat Vincent, he'll quit cracking so many horrible jokes in my face.

"Fine," I say. "On the playground. After school."

"Bring your best stuff, Jamie, because I sure will. I love competition. Speaking of competitions..."

Oh, boy. Here we go.

"Did you hear about the guy who lost his grip at the woodchopping contest? He was de-feeted!"

Nobody in the hallway laughs, except, of course, Vincent O'Neil.

"Get it? De-feeted? The ax slipped and he chopped off—"

"WE GOT IT!" the whole hall shouts.

Oh, man. This comedy competition on the playground? It should be a cakewalk.

Even for me.

Chapter 31

THE BIG LAUGH-OFF

"You can take this guy, Jamie," says my corner man, Gaynor.

"Total knockout!" adds Pierce.

"Go for the funny bone!" says Gilda, who's going to record the whole thing on her iPhone so she can post my schoolyard Comedy Smackdown victory on YouTube.

There's a circle of kids, maybe four deep, ringing the jungle gym. The crowd parts as Vincent O'Neil makes his way into the joke pit, where I'm just sitting, waiting for him.

In a rare mutual decision, Vincent and I have chosen Brightman Kornegay III, our class president, to be the referee and judge. He'll be the human laugh-o-meter and decide which one of us scores the biggest yuks.

"Okay, guys," says Brightman. "Keep it clean. Uh, no hitting below the belt and, um, no Justin Bieber jokes."

We flip a coin. Vincent, who's officially the challenger, calls heads.

"Heads it is," says Brightman. "Pass or play?"

"Oh, I'm playing," says Vincent. "You know, Jamie, you remind me of an Emo Philips joke—because I heard you got some new underwear. Well, it was new to *you*!"

Believe it or not, the crowd laughs like crazy. A very loud—almost mechanical—"Ha-ha-ha!"

"Jamie?" says Brightman. "Your joke."

"Well, I've got this friend. A guy named Joey. They caught him stealing stuff from lockers. Poor guy. I'm wondering what he's going to do with all those magnetic mirrors. I mean, have you seen how some people decorate their lockers?"

"Bor-ing!" shouts someone in the back of the crowd.

Another heckler joins in: "Who cares about your stupid friends or some girl's stupid locker?"

What do they call a boxer who gets beat up in a fight?
A sore loser!
What's green, red, and yellow and wears boxing gloves?
Fruit punch!
What did the boxer say to his barber?
Give me an uppercut!
Quit blocking my jokes with punch lines!

I recognize both voices. Zits and Useless. Stevie Kosgrov's very own goon squad.

They throw me off. I hesitate. Vincent jumps in.

"Hey, today the physics teacher told us that photons have mass. Really? I didn't even know they were Catholic!"

"Now, *that's* comedy!" shouts Stevie Kosgrov at the rear of the crowd. *"Right?"*

He glares. The crowd laughs.

Yes, it's stilted. And forced. But it's also very, very loud.

The fix is in. Stevie's pounding his fist into his open palm, encouraging everybody to laugh and cheer for O'Neil. I'm so dumbfounded I just sit there and choke. I can't think of a single funny thing to say.

"What? That's all you've got?" taunts O'Neil. "Hey, have any of you guys met Lamie Jamie's uncle Frankie? He's so old, he shops at *Extremely* Old Navy. I tell you, he's so old, he farts dust. In fact, one time, Jamie's uncle walked into an antiques store and they sold *him*!"

The crowd is chant-laughing now. "HA-HA! HO-HO! HAR-DEE-HAR!" It's like watching soldiers marching in lockstep, doing exactly what they've been ordered to do—or else!

I don't stick around to hear the judge's decision.

I roll past my friends. They look as sad as I feel. Gilda puts away her iPhone.

This is the first time I have ever lost a comedy competition.

Yes, I know it was rigged. And I know my evil bully cousin coerced the crowd into laughing at

Vincent O'Neil's corny jokes. But that doesn't make me feel any better.

In fact, I feel like the biggest loser to ever go to middle school.

Which means the real winner of today's comedy contest wasn't Vincent O'Neil.

It was Stevie Kosgrov.

Chapter 32

RAFE WHAT?

Um, Jamie?
Yeah?
I'm Rafe Khatchadorian.
Gesundheit.
Yeah, I get that a lot.

So how do you spell Khatchadorian?
Very slowly!
...
You know you could've beaten that guy if you'd used some of your funny material instead of just choking.
Yeah. I do that sometimes.
And sweat. I sweat like a lawn sprinkler hooked up to a water buffalo with bladder-control issues.

So, um, are you new here?
Depends. Where exactly are we?
Long Beach Middle School.
I think I took a wrong turn at page fifty-three.
But you couldn't stop and ask for directions because you're a guy.
Exactly.
Mr. Patterson? Mr. Grabber-however-you-say-that? Ms., um, Ms. Illustrator Lady? Any of you? Get me out of here. Please?
Thank you!

Who was that kid you were just talking to?
I don't know, but he felt like my brother from another mother.

THE SCENE OF THE CRIME

The next day, I'm still feeling a little down.

Especially when Vincent O'Neil takes a victory lap in the cafeteria by standing up on a table to host his very own "rebroadcast" of his winning performance.

"And then I said, 'He's so old, he shops at Extremely Old Navy.' Get it? See, Old Navy is the store, but Extremely Old Navy is this store I made up to show how old the guy is. What's the matter, people? Why aren't you laughing?"

"Because Stevie Kosgrov isn't here to threaten them all with knuckle sandwiches," mutters Gilda.

"You ever wonder what a knuckle sandwich would actually taste like?" says Pierce.

"Yeah," I say. "A McRib. But with knuckles."

Gaynor laughs so hard, chocolate milk comes squirting out his nose.

"You've still got it, dude."

"I'm glad you think so, Gaynor."

"The judges up in Boston on Saturday will think so, too," says Gilda. "Stevie won't be up there, threatening them with bodily harm."

"Maybe I should go back to doing jokes from joke books," I say.

In the distance, we can hear Vincent O'Neil.

"Hey—what flies through the air covered in syrup? Peter Pancake! Get it?"

"Then again, maybe not."

★ ★ ★

After school, Gaynor asks Pierce, Gilda, and me to follow him to his locker.

"What for?" I ask.

"Something extremely important to my conscience!"

His *conscience*? Geez! Cue the melodramatic music, please. Thank you.

With the suspense killing us, we follow him down the hall to our lockers, where he pulls out two huge shopping bags he has somehow crammed inside.

"What's that?" I ask.

"The things I stole from all those lockers."

"I'm going to put it all back, except the money. I kind of spent that at the movies. But Uncle Frankie lent me some cash to live on, and I'll work until I earn enough to pay everyone back."

"You washing dishes at the diner?" I ask.

Gaynor shakes his head. "Busing tables."

Gilda pulls a bright blue Smurf head from the bag. "You stole somebody's movie souvenir drink cup?"

"Yeah. I don't know what I was thinking."

"Probably because you weren't."

"Probably."

"A rotten banana?" says Pierce, plucking something black, stinky, and slimy out of bag #2.

"It wasn't rotten when I stole it. Last week."

"Come on, you guys," I say. "Let's just put these things back in front of whatever lockers they were from."

"You'd help me do that?" says Gaynor.

"Hey, you'd do it for me, too. We all mess up sometimes. And besides, it takes guts to say you're sorry. It will also take guts for somebody to eat that banana. Or this bologna sandwich. Exactly how long did it take for the meat to turn green?"

"Let's do the previous owners of the moldy sandwich and banana a favor and chuck 'em," says Gilda.

We all nod and laugh. I wouldn't tell him, but Gaynor looks a little choked up.

Teamwork. It's kind of like having a family.

Chapter 34

BAD KARMA

Saturday morning, I'm up bright and early.

Not because we're leaving for Boston at seven AM.

Because I can't sleep.

It's not just that I'm coming off a humiliating schoolyard defeat by Vincent O'Neil, the worst comic in the world. (If anyone ever wrote a book about him, I'm pretty sure it'd be called *He Not Funny*.)

My fingers still smell like rotten bologna mixed with old bananas, from helping Gaynor return his stolen goods.

Stevie Kosgrov dropped by the diner last night to wish me a happy funeral.

And all that real-life stuff I was going to riff on like Jerry Seinfeld does? All I can hear in my head is a heckler shouting, "Who cares about your stupid friends or some girl's stupid locker?"

If I read my horoscope, it'll probably say, "Today is a good day to hide underneath your bed. You might also consider running away. We hear Mexico is nice this time of year."

I feel like I'm surrounded by bad karma, which isn't a heavy metal hair band from the '80s. It's a dark cloud of destiny hovering over my head. I just know the universe is all set to laugh *at* me, not *with* me.

I have to face facts: Fate has decreed that I will end up a loser with all my dreams becoming as worthless as my legs. It's just a matter of time.

Like before this day is done.

Chapter 35

FATE STINKS

Finally, the alarm goes off.

Six AM.

"Up and at 'em, guys," says Uncle Frankie, flicking on the lights in the spare bedroom, which Gaynor and I are still sharing. "Today's the big day! Boston, here we come!"

"Mr. Frankie?" says Gaynor. "Is it okay if I stay here today and bus tables?"

"You don't want to come with us to the comedy club?"

"Nah. Jamie's going to lose. It's his destiny."

And that's right about where I have to cut this part of the story short.

Because even though Gaynor's comment crushes

me, he's so right.

I totally tank in Boston.

I'm so bad, I half expect the audience to throw me into Boston Harbor with a bunch of tea bags. If Paul Revere were here, he'd be riding his horse up and down the streets, warning people: "Jamie Grimm stinks! Jamie Grimm stinks!"

Even Uncle Frankie deserts me.

He leaves halfway through my fifth knock-knock joke. I hear him saying, "Jamie Grimm? Never met the kid. He's not my nephew, that's for sure. And he's definitely not staying in my spare bedroom. No, sir. Never again."

I come in eleventh out of twelve.

The kid in tenth place told his jokes in Farsi. Without a translator.

The only act I beat is a scruffy monkey from Maine who bugged out his eyes, clanged two cymbals together, and screeched, "You want some of me? You want some of me?"

When comedians flop, they call it dying onstage. Right now, I just wish I could.

NEVER LET 'EM SEE YOU SWEAT

I wake up, covered in flop sweat.

WHEW.

It was just a dream. Except for the sweat.

We're talking Niagara Falls. And that's just my forehead. My clothes cling to me like I'm a soggy shrink-wrapped sandwich.

Guess sleeping in my clothes to save time getting dressed in the morning wasn't such a smart idea.

"You okay?" asks Gaynor from his bed.

"Yeah. Just a little, you know, damp."

"Did you wet the bed?"

"I guess. But not in the, uh, traditional way."

"Say no more. You ready to rock Boston's socks off?"

"That's funny," I say.

"Huh?"

"Boston's baseball team. They're the Red Sox."

"I made a joke?"

"You sure did."

"You can use it if you want to, Jamie."

"Thanks."

The lights flick on. Uncle Frankie is in the doorway.

"You boys ready to roll?"

"Just about," I say. "I need to take a shower and change my clothes."

"Good idea," says Uncle Frankie when he sees how drenched I am.

"And I'm gonna write Jamie a few more jokes," says Gaynor. "About socks."

"Really?"

"Hey," I say. "I'll take all the help I can get. You never know when some cymbal-clanging monkey from Maine will show up to give you a run for your money."

Chapter 37

COMEDY CONVOY

"We're gonna caravan from the diner parking lot," says Uncle Frankie as I roll up the ramp into the back of his van.

Gaynor has already called shotgun and is up front in the passenger seat.

Yes, he's coming to Boston with us. The real Gaynor does not want to hang back and bus tables instead of watching me tank in Boston like dream Gaynor did.

"Um, what exactly do you mean by *caravan*, Uncle Frankie?" I ask.

"You know, like a convoy. We'll take the lead, the Kosgrovs will follow us...."

He means the Smileys. As in Stevie Kosgrov's

whole family, including (unfortunately) Stevie.

"A few of your other fans might follow us, too."

A few?

When we pull into the diner parking lot, *everybody* is there to say good-bye, wish me good luck, or follow us up to Boston.

It is totally overwhelming.

I feel like I'm Long Beach's one-person Little League team heading off to the Little League World Series in Japan or something. Only, people wouldn't drive to Japan. At least not all the way.

I see Gilda Gold and Pierce. They're both carrying posters to cheer me on.

"Do you have room for two more passengers?" Gilda asks Frankie.

"Only if it's you and the Pierce-a-lator!"

"Excellent! I'm going to video the whole thing, Jamie. That way you can study it, like game films, to prep for the semifinals in Las Vegas."

"Uh, first I have to win the regionals. Today."

"Piece of cake. Who's your competition?"

"I don't know. I've been afraid to check the website."

"Well," says Pierce, "since this is the Northeast Regional, I'm certain we can expect a lot of jokes about New England clam chowder, maple syrup, and Ben & Jerry's ice cream. It's from Vermont."

"Hey, Jamie."

Cool Girl is in the parking lot.

"*Ciao*, bro."

Cool Guy, too. He has bed-head hair, with every spiky tip perfectly placed. I figure he spent hours in front of a mirror to look like he just woke up.

"I wish I could come with you guys," says Cool Girl.

"But we're checking out a pickle festival in Brooklyn," adds Cool Guy, flicking at a strand of hair that's pointing the wrong way. "And sampling some locally sourced artisanal cheeses, too."

I just nod. I have no idea what he's talking about.

"Hey, Crip."

Stevie Kosgrov, Zits, and Useless push their way through the crowd. Literally. They shove everybody else out of their path.

"Just so you know," says Stevie, gripping my armrests and leaning in, "I'll be in the audience. Front row. Center seat. I just love to watch you sweat. Plus, I can't wait to see you lose."

Now Gilda shoves Stevie aside.

"Get a life, Kosgrov. You're just jealous."

"Of what?"

"Jamie. Did this many people show up to cheer you on when you were heading off to the Middle School Bully Olympics?"

"Huh? There's no such thing."

"Really?" snaps Gilda, jutting out her hip. "Maybe you're just not good enough to get invited."

Stevie pouts. I smile.

That's usually how it works.

"All right, everybody!" shouts Uncle Frankie. "It's time to shove off! Let's get our champ to Boston!"

And in a spectacular show of support, Gilda Gold whips off the Boston Red Sox cap she wears *all the time*, and puts on a Yankees hat.

"Yep," she says, "for the first time ever, I'm actually cheering for the New York team!"

Chapter 38

GETTING "CREME'D"

The whole ride up (it's four and a half hours from Long Beach to Boston), I'm staring out the window, watching the highway roll by, and freaking out.

That bad dream I had was so vivid. So real.

Was it an omen? A vision of my impending doom?

The ancient Greeks used to have omens all the time. In fact, they had 'em the way we have hamburgers. They'd see signs and symbols everywhere. In birds, tea leaves, Greek salads. If there was a thunderclap from a cloudless sky, that meant Zeus, the big cheese, was cheering them on. If they dreamed about monkeys banging cymbals, they wouldn't go anywhere near Komos's (the god of comedy) Komedy Klub.

Hey, I've read enough mythology books to know one thing: A screeching monkey in the middle of the night always means doom and gloom. Or at least a splitting headache.

We arrive at Nick's Comedy Stop on Warrenton Street a little after noon. Steven Wright, Denis Leary, and all sorts of comics got their starts here.

The folks running the Planet's Funniest Kid Comic Contest tell us that the first round, featuring all twelve contestants, will start at two PM.

The second round will start at five.

Yep. There are going to be *two* stages! I have to do *two* routines.

Or maybe not.

Because you don't make it to the second round unless you're one of the top six in the first.

While Uncle Frankie (and everybody else) heads off to a restaurant called Legal Sea Foods (I guess that means they don't smuggle their clams) for a quick bowl of "chowda," I head backstage to check things out.

And guess who's in the dressing room?

One of my all-time favorite comics—Boston's own Billy Creme. He's wearing the same black leather bomber jacket and white T-shirt he wore in his first HBO special.

You've probably seen or heard Billy Creme in movies. Like that one where he's the night watchman at an art museum where all the paintings come to life and he has that cream-pie fight with the ghost of Vincent van Gogh. Or that cartoon where he's the voice of the octopus in the sunglasses whose catchphrase is "Let me lend you a hand, pal. I've got eight of 'em."

He's also one of the best stand-up comics on the circuit and a major headliner in Las Vegas.

"Excuse me, sir," I say, "I don't mean to gawk, but, well, I'm a big fan. You're one of my idols!"

"Thanks, Jamie."

"You, uh, know my name?"

"Sure thing. Caught a clip of your act on YouTube. Funny, funny stuff. I can see why you won New York."

"Gosh, thank you, Mr. Creme. Coming from you that means the world to me."

"My pleasure, pal. Can't wait to see what you lay down today. I'm rooting for ya."

"Really?"

"Sure. If you're lucky, maybe you'll take third or fourth."

"Huh?"

"Either that, or Mr. Congeniality. Lots of luck with that."

Before I can figure out what just happened, a kid who looks exactly like a Mini-Me version of Billy Creme, down to the bomber jacket and T-shirt, shuffles into the dressing room.

"Hey, Little Willy!" says Billy Creme. "Meet

Jamie Grimm. He's, you know, handicapped."

"No," says snarky Little Willy. "What gave it away, cousin? His wheelchair, or did he show you his IQ test?"

Billy Creme laughs. "Good one, Little Willy."

"Hey, Jamie. Your hair. What's up with that? Are you auditioning to become the Dutch Boy on the paint cans?"

My *former* idol, Billy Creme, is cracking up.

"And what's with that vest? Is it 1974 in here or something? No. Wait. I get it. That's a life jacket to stop you from drowning in your own sweat. Maybe you can use your seat cushion as a flotation device, too!"

I have no idea what to say. A guy I really looked up to just threw me under the bus, and now a mini-version of him is backing the bus up to finish me off.

You know that four-and-a-half-hour drive from Long Beach to Boston?

It's gonna feel a whole lot longer when I head home a loser.

And we haven't even started the first round yet.

Chapter 39

FUNNY MEETING YOU HERE

I'm waiting in the wings, feeling nauseous and wondering why my fingers are tingling while my head is throbbing. Might have something to do with my heart racing along like a jackrabbit that drank way too many Red Bulls.

The first round has already started. Little Willy Creme is onstage, killing big.

"They say that in thirty years, one out of every three American schoolchildren will be obese," Little Willy snarls like he could care less. "The other two will be starving, I guess, because the fat kid ate all the food in the cafeteria. Totally Hoovered out all the serving pans."

The audience is laughing like hyper hyenas.

And then things get even worse.

I see her.

"Hey, Jamie!" she whispers.

It's Judy Nazemetz. She was in the New York State contest with me and was very nice and extremely funny—sort of a Tina Fey Jr. She's also the star of a new Disney Channel sitcom.

But somehow, in the New York State competition, I beat her.

Which leads me to wonder: *What the heck is she doing here?*

"Hey, Judy," I whisper back.

"Guess you're surprised to see me again, huh?"

I do my best *What? Me? Surprised?* face.

"Nah," I say. "You were fantastic at that gig in New York."

"You were funnier. But it turns out the judges got to pick a wild card contestant."

"Really?" I say, wishing my voice hadn't cracked on the *ee* part. "I didn't know that."

"Yeah. Me neither, till last week. My agent got a call from Joe Amodio."

Oh, boy. Joe Amodio is the big-shot executive producer of the whole Planet's Funniest Kid Comic competition.

"It's like that TV show *America's Got Talent*," Judy continues. "All the judges from all the state competitions in the Northeast got together, looked at tapes, and *ta-da*—they picked me to move on to the regionals."

"So you get a second shot?"

"Yeah. Of course I had to *beg* the people at Disney for some time off from the show so I could prep."

"Of course," I say, like I know what it's like to have my own sitcom.

"I just hope I don't bomb."

"You won't," I say.

We smile at each other for a couple of seconds.

Then she gives me a quick peck on the cheek. "Good luck out there, Jamie. Knock 'em dead."

"Ditto!"

She bounds off. So now I have Little Willy and Judy, the girl with her own TV show, to worry about.

Maybe this is why I'm sweating so much.

And why I can't remember a single punch line or setup.

This is not good.

Because Little Willy just finished up and the emcee is calling my name.

Stevie Kosgrov is about to have his fondest dream come true.

He's about to see me die onstage.

Chapter 40

WILL JAMIE CHOKE? FIND OUT NOW!

My mouth is totally dry.

But my forehead and armpits are spritzing like a berserk watering can cursed by an angry garden gnome.

I roll out to center stage and fiddle with the microphone, lowering it and realizing that in my chair, I am even shorter than Little Willy.

A dusty white spotlight is beaming at me from far off in the distance. I sort of wish it were the bright headlight of an oncoming train that could put me out of my misery. But there's one good thing about being up here in the spotlight: It totally blinds you. The audience becomes a murky silhouette of bobbing heads. I can't see Stevie in the front row. Or any of my friends. All I can sense is that there's a beast out there, one that comics call the Audience. And it's a beast I have to slay.

"Uh, hi. I'm Jamie Grimm."

"Woo-hoo!" shouts Gilda, off in the darkness to my right. I recognize her voice. "Go, Jamie!"

"Oh, great," I ad-lib. "My mother's here."

The audience laughs. They don't know my mom is dead, and I'm not about to tell them because, like I said, they're LAUGHING!

I decide to play it safe. Go with the stuff I know works every time I drag it out.

"You see me in this wheelchair and I know what you're thinking. *Man, he must save a ton of money on running shoes.*"

More laughs.

"You know, I have to wonder, couldn't they come up with a better name for this thing?" I point at my wheelchair. "I mean, come on. Wheelchair? How lame is that? Oh, I see. It's a chair. With wheels. We'll call it, oh, I don't know, how about the Wheelchair?"

More laughs.

So I put on a stilted voice with a thick accent like I'm someone who's just learning English. "'Wheelbarrow. Wheelchair. The wheels on the bus go around and around....'"

I do my bit about how great it is to have handicapped parking, even though the guy on the sign always looks like he doesn't get enough to eat.

“Check this out,” I say, holding up a handicapped-parking placard.

“I mean, how does that skinny little pencil neck even support the guy’s bowling ball head? Actually, he looks like one of the little pinhead people you stick in your plastic car when you play the Game of Life. Except his arms come out of his stomach. How handicapped is this dude? And how do we really know it’s not a sign designating parking for people squatting on beanbag chairs?”

Since they’re still chuckling, I take the crowd on a guided tour of what’s inside the hidden world of the handicapped bathroom. “You roll in, a lady offers you hand towels, a guy hands you breath mints. There’s also a Jacuzzi, free snacks, and much fluffier toilet paper.”

Then I do another bit I’ve done before about what the world looks like from my point of view.

"Belt buckles and belly button jewelry. That's what you see when you live your life at waist level. I hope I never go to Texas. Have you seen the bling in some of those cowboy belt buckles? A guy like me could go blind. And trust me, you don't want to be sitting at butt level on Beanie Weenie day in the cafeteria."

I end by talking about my dream wheelchair.

"One of those electronic numbers with the joystick on the handle. That way I can roll up the sidewalk and play *Madden NFL Football* on my Xbox at the same time."

That gets a laugh and applause, so I quit while I'm ahead (or at least not dead).

"Thank you! I'm Jamie Grimm! You guys have been great. But I gotta go. Seriously. Somebody point me toward the bathroom with the Jacuzzi!"

Okay. I know I wasn't great. I might've even broken my own rule and played the pity card—doing an entire set about me and my wheelchair.

I have to admit—I was psyched out by the Return of Judy and Billy Creme's Mini-Me, Little Willy.

And yes, it didn't help that there was a kid from

Maine who actually dressed up like a monkey with cymbals and told insult jokes.

Fortunately, Monkey Boy came in seventh.

And I came in sixth.

Which means I barely squeaked my way into the second round.

Judy Nazemetz and Little Willy?

They were number one and number two.

Chapter 41

NO RISK, NO REWARD

We take a one-hour break between rounds.

"So long, Grimm," says the boy in the monkey costume as he packs up his cymbals. "If you want some of me, you know where to find me. I'll be in the audience. Cheering *against* you."

Yes, reality is definitely starting to feel pretty unreal.

But I'm not dreaming. I'm competing, as Gaynor, my corner man, reminds me when he comes backstage to give me a pep talk.

"Yo, dude. Not bad."

"Not bad?"

"Totally. But you know and I know—you can do a whole lot better."

"What about Judy Nazemetz and Little Willy?"

"They were funny. But, dude, they weren't *Jamie Grimm* funny."

"Seriously?"

"Seriously. If, you know, you can be serious about comedy. Just go for it. Don't hold back. Fly like a bird. A free bird."

And then he diddles out an air guitar solo. (That old Lynyrd Skynyrd song "Free Bird" is Gaynor's favorite.)

I know he's right.

I didn't get this far by playing it safe. Hey, if I wanted safety, I would've never had this crazy idea that, no matter what, I could be a comedian.

So I decide to risk everything.

When round two starts and the emcee calls my name the second time, I go out and do nothing but brand-new material. Stuff I've never tried anywhere. It's a little like doing a high-wire act blindfolded while juggling chain saws. Very scary, but totally thrilling.

I make up a bit about Godzilla moving to the suburbs to become a "sanitation engineer" who guzzles Dumpsters full of garbage and uses his

powers for good instead of evil. That leads me to a tangent about other out-of-work movie monsters.

King Kong gets a job washing skyscraper windows.

"He licks the Empire State Building clean in like two minutes flat. Buffs the windows with his fur. Gives it a good coat of gorilla wax."

Bruce, the shark from *Jaws*, pulls himself together and goes to work for Bubba Gump Shrimp.

Then I start talking about how I can't wait till I'm sixteen and get to go cruising with hot chicks like my hot friend Gilda in my hot red Staaang. I hit the word *hot* a lot. Get into a rhythm.

"Hot cars used to have cool names," I say. "Mustang. Corvette. Thunderbird." I milk each name. Linger on it. "People used to sing songs about those cars. Nowadays? Hello, is anybody writing songs about their Prius?"

I say *Prius* so it sounds sort of prissy and sing a little jingle I make up on the spot.

"*Come see-us, in our Pri-us. Wouldn't want to be-us, in our Pri-us.*"

People are holding their sides, slapping their knees.

"How about that Nissan Cube?" I put on my suave voice. "'Hey, baby. Wanna hop in my Cube? It's so square, it's six squares in one.' And then there's the Chevy Avalanche. A car that sounds like it's falling apart before you even buy it…"

The audience is laughing so hard, I don't really even hear them anymore.

I *feel* them. It's like I'm a surfer riding the waves, shooting the curls, almost wiping out, but fighting to hang on to my board.

It's basically great.

When I'm done, I can't remember half the stuff I riffed about.

But apparently, it was pretty good.

"You were awesome!" says Judy Nazemetz when she hugs me the second I roll offstage. "It's gotta be down to you or Little Willy."

"Yeah. He was funny. But so were you."

She shrugs. "Meh. Maybe. But, Jamie?"

"Yeah?"

"You funnier!"

Chapter 42

AND THE WINNER IS...

Turns out, Judy was wrong.

She comes in second. Little Willy is third.

And yes—that means what you think it means.

I *won*!

Thanks to totally winging my round-two performance, I am officially crowned the Planet's Funniest Kid Comic Contest's Northeast Regional Champion. I'm moving on to the semifinals in Las Vegas, just like Gilda said I would. And so is Judy Nazemetz. There are eight regions in the competition. Each one sends its top two comedians to Las Vegas for the semifinals. The judges also get to pick two of their favorite losers for Vegas wild card slots.

But that's not what's worrying me right now.

I just remembered. I called Gilda a hot chick in my act. I wonder if she heard me say it?

Uh, *duh*. Of course she did. I had a microphone!

I hope she wasn't offended. I wonder if Gilda even knows how cute she is? I also wonder if I should be thinking this kind of stuff right now, especially without first getting permission from Pierce and Gaynor, my partners on the triple date.

"We was robbed!"

Billy Creme and his Mini-Me rudely interrupt all my Gilda thoughts. They have stomped onstage and are shouting at the panel of judges seated in the front row.

"Willy was way funnier than Nazemetz and Grimm combined!" shouts Billy Creme, whose next movie I'm pretty sure I'm going to skip.

"Way funnier," echoes Little Willy. "How could you pick those two over me? You people are so dumb, you're like an experiment in artificial stupidity!"

"See?" says Cousin Billy. "He's still being funny."

"And you?" Little Willy points to the judge in the middle. "If your brain was made of chocolate, it wouldn't fill an M&M."

For whatever reason, I roll onstage.

The spotlight swings over to me.

"Um, wouldn't that just be an M?" I shrug. "Just saying."

And I roll offstage.

First the audience cracks up. Then they start to chant.

"Jay-mee, Jay-mee!"

I can hear Gilda leading the cheer. And Gaynor and Pierce and Uncle Frankie and Aunt Smiley and…

No.

Stevie Kosgrov?

"Jay-mee!"

Yep. That's him.

"Our decision is final," says the head judge in a dull drone, like he just woke up. When he stands, I recognize the curly tangle of wispy hair under his baseball cap.

It's Steven Wright! One of my comic heroes and a Boston local!

"Now, if you'll excuse me," he says, "my watch is three hours slow and I can't fix it. So I'm moving to Los Angeles." Then he peers over to the wings. Squints. We make eye contact. "Good luck in Las Vegas, Jamie. You too, Judy. I'll be there doing my act at the Orleans. It's kind of a magic show. I have the power to levitate birds. But no one cares."

Awesome! Steven Wright totally talked to me!

And that wasn't even the best part of the night.

This was:

Chapter 43

HOMETOWN HERO

Monday morning, back at school, it seems I have risen to full-blown celebrity status.

Instead of shaking people down in the hallways, Stevie Kosgrov is selling "official" Jamie Grimm whoopee cushions.

"He sat on each and every one. In his wheelchair, people!" he cries like a carnival barker. "Check it out. Jamie Grimm funny fart balloons. The toot that's a hoot."

Talk about awkward. Teachers, even some I have never met, act like I'm their favorite student of all time.

The local TV news is here, too, interviewing people.

"Oh, I always knew Jamie Grimm was destined for greatness," the principal says into a reporter's microphone. "I figured he'd be famous long before he left Long Beach Middle School."

Really? Wow.

Now Mrs. Kressin, the drama club adviser, who's a little flaky and dresses like she might be an elf on weekends, comes up to me.

"Be not afraid of greatness, James," she says

very, well, dramatically. "Some are born great, some achieve greatness, and some have greatness thrust upon them whilst in the Athens of America treading the boards."

"Huh?" I say.

"Don't worry, I speak Shakespeare," says geekmeister Pierce, stepping in to translate. "Mrs. Kressin just said you're awesome because of what you did up in Boston."

"Oh. Thanks!"

I pump Mrs. Kressin's hand. She curtsies. I guess that's what an elfin princess would do.

A lot of the teachers want to tell me their favorite jokes. To be honest, I don't write any of them down in my notebook.

All in all, it's a great way to start the new week.

Until lunchtime, when Vincent O'Neil shows up in the cafeteria.

"Sorry I couldn't catch your act in Boston, Grimm. I was busy. Organizing my toenail clippings. I guess you won on the sympathy vote, huh?"

"No," says Gilda, blood rising to her cheeks in my defense. "He won because, unlike you, Jamie is funny."

"Really? Well, here are a couple of cripple jokes I'm working into my act. Figure I could go onstage with a pair of crutches."

"For the last time, Vincent—"

He cuts Gilda off.

"What do you call a woman with one leg?"

"Ilene," grunts Gaynor.

"What? You've heard it before. Did you steal my Ilene joke, Grimm?"

"Why would anybody steal a joke that horrible?" asks Pierce.

"Yeah," says Gilda. "Why don't you make like a tree and leave?"

"Oh, oh, oh!" O'Neil sputters. "You stole that one, too?"

And finally, for the first time ever, our whole table actually cracks up because of something Vincent O'Neil said.

COOL NEWS

On our way home from school, Gilda fills me in on all the latest school gossip.

And then she drops a bombshell.

"Suzie Orolvsky and Malibu Ken are no longer an item."

"Who?"

"That new kid from California. Ethan Prettyboy. He and Suzie are over."

Okay, I know I shouldn't feel this way, but I am suddenly deliriously happy. If Cool Girl has broken up with her Hollywood hunk, maybe I have a chance. Maybe we'll even kiss again.

"Apparently," Gilda continues, "Suzie *really* wanted to hop on a train and come see you up in

Boston on Saturday. But Ethan didn't want to miss that picklefest in Brooklyn."

"Wow," I say. "I can't believe Cool Girl and Cool Guy broke up."

"Who're these cool people?"

"That's what I call Suzie and Ethan." I tap my head. "In my mind."

"Oh." A queasy frown wiggles across Gilda's face. "You think she's cool?"

"I guess. Yeah. I mean, the way she acts. The way she looks. The way—"

"Okay, okay. I get it. She's Cool Girl."

And I'm Dumb Boy. I've hurt Gilda's feelings.

"You're cool, too," I say, without thinking.

(Note to self: Next time, think.)

Before I can explain, Gilda turns away.

"This is my corner. Have a great night, Jamie. Congratulations on being the most famous person to ever go to Long Beach Middle School."

And she basically runs away.

Girls. They make being a guy very, very difficult. Sort of like being on the bomb squad. Do I snip the red wire or the blue wire or just wait and see what blows up in my face next?

I decide to take a little detour and head over to the boardwalk to think about how I can fix things up with Gilda, who really is a great girl friend—as in, a friend who is also a girl.

But then I see her.

Cool Girl. Sitting all by herself on what I like to call our kissing bench.

She looks so sad.

"Hey," I say.

"Hey."

"You okay?"

"Not really."

"You want to talk about it?"

"Not really."

"Okay."

And we just sit there, not talking to each other, for like fifteen minutes.

And then Suzie says, "You're nice, Jamie."

"So are you."

"Not according to Ethan."

"Well, what does he know? He goes to pickle festivals. I hear he drools whenever somebody says the word *gherkin*."

Suzie smiles. And then she laughs.

We don't kiss. Or hold hands. Or say much else.

But I think Suzie is glad I dropped by the boardwalk. I guess even Cool Girls get the blues.

And it's a comedian's job to chase those blues away.

Chapter 45

MAD ABOUT MADISON AVENUE

Uncle Frankie and I hold a strategy session for the semifinals in Las Vegas.

We decide I need to broaden my horizons, to take in some new experiences so I can develop a ton of fresh material.

"Face it, kiddo," says Uncle Frankie. "You got lucky winging it up in Boston. To win out in Vegas against the best of the best, you're gonna need to bring your A game and a trunkload of new routines. Lucky for you, I know somebody who can get us into the perfect place to work on some new material."

Turns out one of Uncle Frankie's regulars at the diner has a nephew who works in—medieval trumpet fanfare, please—advertising! A comic gold mine. "He's what they call an account executive at J. Walter Thompson, one of the biggest ad agencies in the world. And since this coming Friday is a school holiday, we're going to his office in the city."

"What's an account executive do?" I ask.

Uncle Frankie shrugs. "Nobody really knows, Jamie. But they all wear suits, so it must be something important. And probably hilarious."

Friday morning, we hop on the Long Island Rail Road and head into Manhattan.

J. Walter Thompson's New York offices are on Lexington Avenue, even though everybody thinks the entire advertising business is on Madison Avenue. (And that's why, Uncle Frankie explains, some people refer to the whole industry as Madison Avenue. Maybe they need a new map.)

Anyway, the offices look like a really cool futuristic hotel on the moon, with lots of bright colors and glass-walled meeting rooms that remind me of goldfish bowls. Without the water. Or the fish.

And Uncle Frankie is right—the place is truly hilarious (even though I don't think the people working there know it).

In one conference room, extremely intense people

sit around a table and point at charts. They're saying super-serious stuff about fast-food joints, which they call QSRs. It stands for Quick Service Restaurants…or Quality Sure Reeks. One of those.

In another room, creative people in blue jeans and lumberjack shirts are presenting a storyboard (they told me it's kind of like a comic strip that shows what a TV commercial might look like) to several people in suits.

The people in suits are frowning.

“I don’t know. Do we really want to say our new skin moisturizer for pets is the cat’s meow? Won’t that offend the dogs in our target audience?”

“We could focus-group it,” suggests an account executive with gray hair.

“We sure could,” says an assistant account executive with no hair.

“Focus groups are good,” says a junior account coordinator with a whole head of hair.

“We love focus groups,” say all the clients.

The two creative types holding the storyboard look like they might cry.

A focus group, I find out, is where a bunch of average, ordinary people talk about a product or what’s wrong with a commercial while advertising people watch them from behind a one-way mirror and take notes.

But what’s really funny about advertising is how serious everybody is—especially about trucks and cars. J. Walter Thompson has a small test track on the top floor, where cars and pickups zip around while company writers try to come up with new words for *fast* or *rugged*.

These people are even serious about acne cream.

SORT EXTREME
Look, it's green. Like your boogers.
Heh, heh, yeah.
Dude, I just recycled you.
Good respondents.
Respondents suck.
This sucks.

"We're not selling pimple remover," says a lady in a business suit. "We're selling confidence in a tube."

Hey, if that's what acne cream can do for a guy, sign me up. I could use some confidence in a tube in Las Vegas.

I wonder if it works on armpits, too?

Chapter 46

AND IN OTHER NEWS...

I'm cranking away like crazy on my Vegas routines, filling brand-new notebooks with ideas and jumping-off points. For instance, confidence in a tube. I could riff on that for hours. I mean, what else could they put in a tube? Happiness? Boredom? Oh, wait. Boredom in a tube is TV....

Fortunately, Gilda has volunteered to help me turn my material into what she calls solid gold.

Yes, she has forgiven me for my Cool Girl goof-up.

Or maybe she remembers how I (in a fit of improvisational fury) called her hot onstage in Boston. Maybe hot is better than cool when you're a girl.

Anyway, I'm glad Gilda is in my corner. She's a pretty good critic and coach.

"Okay," Gilda says one day after school, "let's look at what Letterman and Leno do."

"Well, they usually come out and do a monologue of jokes at the start of their shows."

"Exactly. And what's the monologue about?"

"I dunno. Stuff. Whatever happened that day."

Gilda touches a finger to her nose. "Bingo. Current events." She pulls a newspaper out of her backpack. "You ever hear of a comedian named Mort Sahl?"

"Sure. Instead of doing one-liners, he'd just walk onstage with that day's newspaper and go."

Gilda hands me the paper. "Go!" she says.

"Really?"

"Go."

"This is the Style section...."

"Go!"

"Okay." I scan the headlines.

MODEL WEARS MOST UNFLATTERING DRESS EVER

And I go.

"I don't know if you people heard about this demon dress in New York City. Apparently, it came alive and started saying stuff like 'Yes, I make you look fat. I also make you look dumb. Why dumb? Because you're wearing me, the most unflattering dress ever.'"

Gilda's grinning her face off. "Exactly. Just do that a couple of times a day," she suggests. "Find a random headline and do something wacky with it."

"Okay. What else?"

"Phineas and Ferb," says Gilda. "Beavis and Butt-Head. What makes these people funny?"

"Well, for one thing, they're not people. They're cartoons."

"More, please."

"Well, Beavis and Butt-Head are like a pair of six-year-olds trapped inside the bodies of teenagers."

"You mean they're idiots."

"Yeah. That's why they're funny. Everybody thinks they're smarter than two idiots like Beavis and Butt-Head."

Gilda nods. "They're rude and ugly idiots, too."

"That's even funnier. Beavis and Butt-Head say whatever's on their minds with no editing. Just like Cool Girl."

Gilda rolls her eyes. "Again with the Cool Girl?"

"No, I'm just saying..."

"What? Suzie Orolvsky would be the 'hot chick' in your 'hot red Staaang' instead of me if you knew how to pronounce her last name?"

I smile.

For one thing, it's nice to know Gilda remembers what I said about her in Boston.

For another, she just gave me an awesome idea for a bit.

"That's great," I say.

"What?"

"Picking a girlfriend based on how easy it is to pronounce her name. I mean, it's hard enough for guys to call girls without getting all tangled up trying to say their names. 'Uh, hello, is this, uh, Onyi Nwokeji? Er, Onyay Nowaykeyjee. Onion Nwookiee.' Or what if they have a horrible last name and you have to meet their parents? 'Oh, hello, Mr. and Mrs. Buttington. Fanny has told me so much about you.'"

Gilda's laughing and shaking her head. "Fanny Buttington? That's just dumb."

"Yep," I say proudly. "Beavis-and-Butt-Head dumb."

Chapter 47

SPEAKING OF DUMB...

In the middle of my intense training for Las Vegas, Long Beach Middle School decides to toss a monkey wrench into my well-oiled comedy machine.

And by monkey wrench, I mean report card.

It's not close to what it should be, unless you have a fondness for the third and fourth letters of the alphabet.

"Ha!" says Stevie when he sees all the Cs and Ds lined up in a tidy grid. "You're supposed to be tutoring *me*?"

Even worse, my "effort" grades are pretty crummy, too.

Uncle Frankie shakes his head when I show it to him.

His yo-yo stops spinning. Just kind of droops sadly on its string.

"This is bad, Jamie."

"I know. But, well, I've been focusing on my act and—"

"You should've been focusing on your schoolwork, too. They call that multitasking. Like flipping burgers while looping-the-loop. To make it in this world, kiddo, you've got to be able to handle more than one thing at a time. I don't like doing this, but...Jamie, you're grounded."

I have never seen Uncle Frankie look so disappointed in me.

"Are you taking back the Mustang, too?"

"No. Not yet, anyway. But no more comedy rehearsals, no more field trips to scout out new material, no more nothing—not until you buckle down and get these grades up."

To make it official, we pay a visit to the Smileys.

"I agree with your uncle Frankie, Jamie," says Mrs. Smiley. "And I'm speaking for Mr. Kosgrov, too."

"How about Ol' Smiler?" I ask. "Does the dog get a vote? Because I think he might be on my side. I used to let him lick my gruel bowl."

Nobody laughs.

Not even Ol' Smiler. He kind of groans and flops on the floor with a disappointed sigh.

That night, Uncle Frankie comes into my room for a man-to-man talk.

"Look, Jamie, you probably think we're all being pretty hard on you. But getting good grades is your primary job right now. It's your meat and potatoes. Doing comedy, performing in Vegas, that's the extra stuff. The gravy."

"But comedy is my life."

"I know. And when you have a dream, you should chase after it with everything you've got. But, and this is a very big but..."

(I would've laughed at that *very big but* except I'm not supposed to be thinking about comedy or butt jokes until my grades improve.)

"…even when you're dreaming, you need to take care of your primary responsibilities. Okay?"

"Okay."

"Good. I'm glad we had this little talk."

"Uncle Frankie?"

"Yeah?"

"The Las Vegas semifinals are only four weeks away."

"Good. You have a whole month to turn some of those Cs and Ds into As and Bs."

"And if I don't?"

Uncle Frankie pauses, then shakes his head. "No Vegas, kiddo. Sorry."

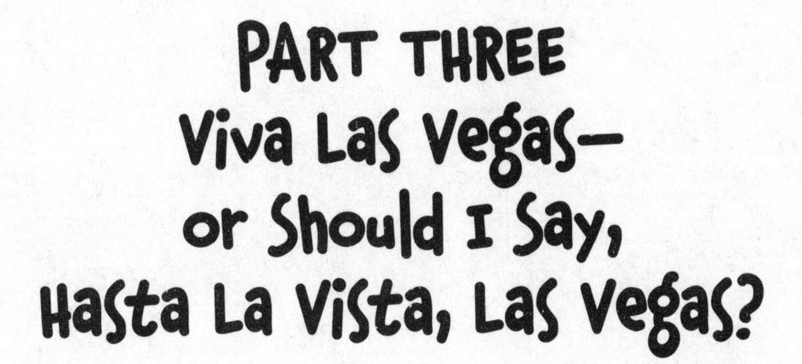

PART THREE
Viva Las Vegas— or Should I Say, Hasta La Vista, Las Vegas?

Chapter 48

NOSE-TO-THE-GRINDSTONE TIME

For the next three weeks, it's *all* schoolwork, *all* the time.

I try not to think funny thoughts. I put down the joke books and pick up the textbooks. I don't even read the funny pages in the Sunday newspaper.

Cramming for my American history exam, I realize I now know a bunch of stuff that I'll probably forget the day after I take the test. Like the names of every president of the United States in order (plus the fact that Warren G. Harding's middle name was Gamaliel). I'm not sure how much more I can squeeze into my brain at this point.

I'm also pushing Stevie Kosgrov like crazy, trying

to drag him across the finish line from an F to maybe a C- or a D+.

Stevie does not wish to be dragged. In fact, he is still threatening me with serious bodily harm.

"Don't even think about making me think, Grimm. It hurts my head."

I try to explain to Stevie that his brain is like any other muscle. "Sure, it'll be sore when you use it for the first time. But the more you work with it, the less pain you'll feel."

And then Stevie explains all the pain he is planning to inflict on my head. With his fists.

But we both need to ace our semester exams for me to make it to Las Vegas. Stevie's parents, my legal guardians, are the ones who have to sign the consent form for me to take the flight out west and appear on TV. That's right: The semifinals of the Planet's Funniest Kid Comic competition will be a television show like *America's Got Talent* or *American Idol*. Millions of people will be watching.

So I keep pushing.

"Okay, Stevie, memorize this sentence: *How I wish I could calculate pi.*"

"Why?"

"It'll help you remember the first decimals of pi."

"Oh, yeah? How?" He cracks his knuckles.

"The number of letters in each word corresponds to a digit in pi: three one four one five nine two."

I think Stevie is actually taking it in. I can see his lips moving.

"Here's another: *I Viewed Xerxes Loping Carelessly Down Mountains*. That gives you the order of Roman numerals: I, V, X, L, C, D, M."

Because I make studying a game where Stevie learns a few tricks that'll help him beat the test and his teachers, he actually starts getting into it.

Pretty soon, he's teaching me.

"*King Henry Doesn't Usually Drink Chocolate Milk*," says Stevie.

I just nod. To ask him what he's talking about would mean risking my life.

"That's how you memorize the basic prefixes in the metric system, dummy," says Stevie. "Kilo, hecto, deca, units, deci, centi, milli."

"Um, what are *units*?"

"Meters, grams, or liters, you idiot!"

Yes, the pupil has become the teacher.

And I might actually have a milli-chance of going to Las Vegas!

Chapter 49

STOP AND SMELL THE SEA SPRAY

The night before my big semester exams, I decide to give my brain a break.

I've crammed it so full of facts and figures it's like a suitcase you have to sit on to close. I need to inhale some salty air instead of my study buddy Stevie's BO.

So I roll down to the boardwalk.

Guess who's sitting on what used to be our bench?

(Well, okay, she would be the only one actually sitting on the bench when it was "our bench," but I used to park my chair right next to it.)

Looks like Cool Girl is taking a break, too, staring up at the twinkling stars.

"Hey," she says when she hears my wheels squeaking up beside her. (Note to self: WD-40 the axles *soon*.)

"Hi," I say. "How's it going?"

"Not bad. How about you?"

I shrug. "I dunno. My head is so full of history and math I think it might explode."

"Like in a cartoon?"

"Yeah. BOOM! There goes the Mason-Dixon Line dividing the middle colonies from the Southern colonies. POW! I no longer know the difference between an isosceles trapezoid and a rhombus."

"*Rhombus* is a funny-sounding word," says Cool Girl.

"Definitely." I slip into my smooth dude voice. "'Wow, check out the rhombus on that girl.'" Then I shift back to me. "Though *trapezoid* is pretty comical, too. Sounds like a race of aliens invading the earth. 'Run for your life! The Trapezoids just landed....'"

Cool Girl chuckles in that extremely cool way she has of letting me know I tickled her funny bone.

"I miss you, Jamie," she says.

"I miss you, too."

Hey, I can't help it. I still like her.

"Sorry about you and Ethan," I say.

"I'm not. The dude was a total poser."

"Really? I guess that's why he always looked like he was posing for a J.Crew catalog." I do my best slouch in the chair, cock a hand on my hip, and pout out my lips.

Cool Girl laughs again. "We can still be friends, right, Jamie?"

"Sure. We don't need to kiss and stuff."

"Of course not," says Cool Girl. "Kissing and stuff just complicates everything."

I'm nodding. "Definitely. Why ruin a friendship to, basically, moisten our lips? That's why they invented ChapStick."

"I agree. Just being friends is totally cool."

And then Cool Girl reaches over to take my hand.

"Is this what friends do?" I ask.

"Sometimes," says Cool Girl.

"And then do they kiss?"

"No. At least not tonight."

Yes, life can sure be confusing. But hopefully it will never get any crazier than middle school, which, in my opinion, has got to be the craziest time in anybody's life.

Chapter 50

FAMILY TIME

All the studying pays off.

I ace my exams. My grades are back in familiar territory: the land of As and Bs.

Stevie? He has, at long last, become average—a solid C student. Okay, C-minus, but come on, it's the letter that really counts.

My buddy Pierce (the genius) scored 100s on all his tests except math, where he got a 105 because he knew the answer to the bonus question and could name all twenty-one prime numbers between 100 and 200.

Gaynor was another solid C citizen and told us he would be spending the weekend taking care of his mom, who was coming home from the cancer treatment center after her final round of chemotherapy. Gilda, Pierce, and I volunteered to help out, but Gaynor said he and his mom needed some "alone" time.

I think he's going to finally tell her about the locker burglaries.

Anyway, on Saturday morning, one week before the semifinals, Mr. and Mrs. Smiley sign all the paperwork required for me to fly off to Las Vegas with Uncle Frankie—on Thursday.

That's in five days!

"I haven't been to Vegas since Caesars Palace hosted the World Yo-Yo Olympics," Uncle Frankie says as we cruise up the highway for a Sunday drive in his Mustang with the top down and the radio blaring.

"When was that?" I ask.

"Long, long time ago, kiddo. I was in high school. Your grandparents took me and your dad."

"Did my dad like to yo-yo, too?"

"Not really. But he was my cheering section."

Frankie hums along to the 1950s doo-wop music pumping out of the speakers. We're celebrating my good grades and, according to Frankie, my

JUDGES
100m YO-YO HURL
You need a really long string for this part of the competition.

"upcoming victory in Vegas." We stowed my wheelchair in the back and just took off.

"So where are we going?" I ask when we cross the George Washington Bridge and head up the Palisades Parkway on the New Jersey side of the Hudson River.

"I dunno," says Uncle Frankie. "I thought maybe we'd go say hi to your mom and dad and little Jenny. Let them know how good you're doing."

Okay. That puts a lump in my throat.

He means we're on our way to Saint Thomas Cemetery, just north of Cornwall, my old hometown.

When we reach the cemetery, Uncle Frankie helps me transfer into my chair. We make our way across the rutted cemetery lawn, weaving around headstones and marble monuments.

We reach a shiny grave marker with four names etched into the smooth gray stone. Three of the names have two dates listed beneath them—the birth and death dates of my mother, father, and sister. Their death dates, of course, are all the same.

One name only has its year of birth and a dash.

That would be mine.

Someday, I guess, in whatever year I die, I will

be buried up here in the Grimm family plot. They'll chisel in the year of my death after that little dash. The headstone will be complete.

Uncle Frankie bows his head and says a silent prayer.

Me? I'm thinking about that dash. When I'm gone, that's all that'll really matter—what I did during that short little squiggle between the two dates: the dash that represents my entire life.

Yes, as weird as it may seem when you're a kid stuck in middle school, life is short. Trust me. I know this from experience. My sister, Jenny, never even made it this far.

Uncle Frankie rests his hand on my shoulder.

I bow my head and say my own silent prayer:

Hey, Mom and Dad. Jenny. Things are going okay. Uncle Frankie and the Smileys are looking out for me. My grades are good again, too. Cousin Stevie's...well, let's just say he's not flunking. Oh, by the way—I know heaven is pretty awesome, with all sorts of incredible stuff to do, but if you get the chance, think about me every once in a while, okay? I can feel it when you do.

Honest. I can.

I miss you guys.
Hope you miss me.

BEWARE THE MIGHTY MEATY

After visiting the cemetery, Uncle Frankie and I grab a quick lunch at the Fiddlestix Cafe on Main Street in Cornwall.

I recognize a few kids in the restaurant. Former classmates.

When I wave at them, a couple wave back. Then the adults with them start whispering behind their hands at each other.

I can't hear what they're saying, but I know what they're talking about.

Me. My wheelchair. "The accident."

"So, kiddo," says Uncle Frankie when he sees the sad look on my face, "what's good here?"

"The burgers, I guess."

Uncle Frankie makes a funny scowling face. "Are they as good as mine?"

I can't help smiling. "No way."

"Well, we should check 'em out. Size up my competition."

So we both order the Build a Mighty Meaty.

That means we'll be wolfing down half-pound burgers served with fries *and* onion rings. I top mine with lettuce, tomato, and American cheese. Uncle Frankie goes with bacon, mayonnaise, and three kinds of cheese: mozzarella, cheddar, and Swiss.

I think he's doing top-secret research for the diner. Seeing how much cheese a cheeseburger can take before basically becoming a grilled cheese sandwich with meat sprinkles.

For dessert, we both go with the coconut cupcakes with coconut cream frosting topped with toasted coconut.

After lunch, we hit the road again.

Frankie loads in another CD filled with 1950s rock-and-roll tunes.

And of course, he sings along.

We're back on Long Island in no time. Well, that's

how it feels, because we're having so much fun.

"Come on, Jamie," Uncle Frankie says when a group called the Chords starts crooning a doo-wop classic. "Sing along with me!"

Easier said than done.

Frankie starts out. *"Hey nonny ding dong, alang alang alang, boom ba-doh, ba-doo ba-doodle-ay..."*

Yes, those are the real lyrics.

"Do the sh-booms!" Frankie cries out. And he

sings, "*Oh, life could be a dream...*"

I say "Sh-boom!"

"*If I could take you up in paradise up above!*"

I say "Sh-boom!" again.

Before long, we're both trying to keep up with the tumbling harmonies without laughing too hard. It's a little like musical yo-yoing.

Yes, Uncle Frankie is a nut. He's also the best uncle anybody ever had and probably my best friend in the whole world.

Just being with him is a blast.

But suddenly, the singing stops. So does the music.

Frankie's finger is on the Eject button. The slim silver disc slides out of the dashboard CD player.

"Oof," he says. His forehead is dappled with sweat. "I don't feel so good."

He puts a fist to his gut. "Must've been that burger bomb I ate. Whooo. Good thing we're almost home."

I agree.

A few minutes later, Uncle Frankie says he doesn't feel so good again.

Trust me: He doesn't *look* so good, either.

Chapter 52

CARSICK

oof.”

As we pull into Long Beach, Frankie really starts to feel sick.

Really, really sick.

"I've got agita like you wouldn't believe."

"What's agita?" I ask.

"Heartburn."

Uncle Frankie eases the car over to the side of the road.

His breathing is hard and fast, like he just ran a marathon or something.

"Uncle Frankie? Are you okay?"

"Gimme a minute, kiddo." He mops at the sweat beading up on his brow. "I'm freezing and sweating at the same time. Go figure."

"Maybe we should call a doctor," I say.

"Nah. It's just heartburn. I'll feel fine in a second. Soon as this elephant climbs off my chest. Oof."

And then he slumps forward, his chin resting against the steering wheel.

"Uncle Frankie? Uncle Frankie!" I shout.

I'm not a doctor, but I'm starting to think he's having a heart attack, right here in his Mustang convertible.

I start digging around in his jacket pockets. His pants pockets. The glove compartment.

Finally, I find his cell phone.

I call 911.

The dispatcher says help is on the way.

I tell them to hurry. Please!

"Hang on, Uncle Frankie," I say through my tears.

I wish I could do something more. I wish I could run up the street and get help. Or drive him to an emergency room. Or drag him out of the car and give him CPR.

But I can't do any of those things.

My legs won't let me.

So I sit there and tell Uncle Frankie to hang on. Help is on the way.

I say another prayer. Ask my dad to look out for his big brother.

And then I move in as close as I can and start singing. Softly. Right in Uncle Frankie's ear.

"Oh, life could be a dream (sh-boom)..."

I skip the bit about paradise up above.

I need Uncle Frankie down here.

Chapter 53

EVEN A BAD JOKE IS GOOD MEDICINE

You'd think that after spending so much time in hospitals, I wouldn't freak out about certain things.

You'd be wrong.

I'm beyond scared, all the way to terrified.

Uncle Frankie has been moved from the emergency room to what they call the intensive care unit.

Been there. Done that.

The ICU isn't exactly the happiest place on earth. Lots of beeping monitors and dripping tubes and frowning nurses.

Fortunately, I'm not alone in the waiting area. Everybody is there with me. The Smileys. Gaynor and Pierce. Gilda Gold and Cool Girl. Even Vincent O'Neil shows up.

An extremely serious young doctor in scrubs comes out to see us.

"Are you Frank Grimm's family?"

"Yes," says Aunt Smiley.

"He's my uncle," I say.

"And," says Gaynor, "he's an extremely cool dude."

The doctor nods. "Mr. Grimm had a mild heart attack. One of his coronary arteries was blocked by cholesterol-rich plaque that had been building up on the artery's walls."

Apparently, the ginormous burger and mountain of greasy fries we ate up in Cornwall pushed Uncle Frankie over his lifetime artery gunk limit and caused the cholesterol walls to come a-tumblin' down.

"We're going to do an angioplasty."

The cardiologist quickly explains how he's going to snake a tube up into Uncle Frankie's heart artery so they can blow up a balloon and unclog the blocked blood vessel. Great. My uncle is going to have a birthday party in his chest. Maybe a float from the Macy's Thanksgiving Day parade. I hope they give him Kermit the Frog or Snoopy.

While Uncle Frankie has his procedure (because everything they do to you in a hospital is called a procedure), the rest of us wait.

And wait.

And wait.

Vincent O'Neil tries to lighten the mood in the waiting room with a corny joke.

It goes over like a loud fart at a funeral.

"That joke is horrible, Vincent," says Cool Girl.

"Yeah. I know," says Vincent, very humbly. "I just thought it might, you know, remind us all that there are worse things in this world than a heart attack."

"Like your jokes?" says Pierce.

"Exactly."

And somehow, we're suddenly all laughing and smiling. We're also surprised to discover that Vincent "The Joke Machine" O'Neil is actually human.

"So you want to hear the one about the old lady and the bad hospital food?"

"No!" all of us say at once. And then we start laughing again.

Hey, didja hear the one about the guy who had a serious accident? When he woke up in the ER he started shouting, "Doctor! I can't feel my legs!" And the doctor said, "Of course you can't. I cut your arms off!"
EMPATHY FOR DUMMIES

The heart doctor reappears while we're in the middle of our giggle fit and says, "I guess you already heard the good news."

"No," says Aunt Smiley.

"What's up, Doc?" asks Uncle Smiley.

"Mr. Grimm is going to be okay. He'll need to take it easy for a while, of course. Stick close to home and lay off the fatty foods. But he's going to be okay."

And then the doctor starts giggling.

Because all of us are hugging him, and group hugs kind of tickle.

ALL HANDS ON DECK

While Uncle Frankie recuperates from his "mild heart attack," I move back in with the Smileys.

Be it ever so humble, there's no place like my garage.

Of course, the whole experience with Uncle Frankie has given me more material for my act. For instance, how can a heart attack be "mild"? Are heart attacks like salsa? Do they come in different strengths? Mild, spicy, and deadly?

And those balloons they put inside people's chests. Do they twist them first to make 'em look like poodles? That'd make for funnier X-rays.

Anyway, with Uncle Frankie out of commission for a couple of weeks, Mr. and Mrs. Smiley have taken over for him at the diner. They're keeping the restaurant running *and* keeping up with their regular lives and jobs. Even Ol' Smiler is busy. Someone has to clean up the food people drop on the floor.

The only thing Mr. and Mrs. Smiley aren't doing very much of these days is sleeping. And I have to say, I am impressed.

They're actually pretty cool.

Well, maybe *cool* isn't exactly the right word. They're solid. Dependable. Hardworking.

And I'm counting on them to let me go to Vegas on my own.

Chapter 55

CALLING IT QUITS

On Monday, when we're supposed to fax all our final paperwork to the folks at the Planet's Funniest Kid Comic competition, Aunt Smiley and I have a little heart-to-heart chat between school and my dinner shift at the diner, where I'm manning the cash register.

"Jamie?" she says, with a look on her face I can only call grim.

"Yeah. I know what you're going to say."

"I'm sorry." Tears start welling up in her eyes.

"That's okay," I say, because I don't want to make her feel any worse about having to choose Uncle Frankie's well-being over my dreams. Heck, I'd choose Uncle Frankie, too. If we don't all pitch in at the diner, the restaurant will most likely go out of business while Frankie's stuck at home recuperating.

"Hey," I say, "maybe they'll do the comedy contest again next year."

Aunt Smiley sniffles back her tears. "You're right, Jamie. Maybe they will. That'd be great. And you'd win, Jamie. I know you would."

So we call the contest's headquarters together. Let them know that I, Jamie Grimm, am officially withdrawing from the competition taking place this coming Saturday afternoon at the Laugh Factory Comedy Club inside the Tropicana Las Vegas hotel.

Yep, six days away from the biggest performance and audience of my life, I quit.

I also make all Little Willy Creme's dreams come true.

Because by dropping out of the competition, I'm giving him my slot.

Chapter 56

SATURDAY NIGHT DEAD

Saturday night at the diner, we change the channel on the TV from the ball game to the big show out in Las Vegas.

All my friends and family are clustered at the counter, sipping sodas and nibbling French fries.

"You okay?" Gilda asks when I lock my wheels and stare up at the plasma screen mounted on the wall.

"Yeah. I just wish Uncle Frankie were here."

"Me too," says Stevie Kosgrov, hustling out of the kitchen with a tray loaded down with plates of food. "This meat loaf weighs a ton!"

Yes, even Stevie is pitching in and waiting tables. If you don't give him a good tip, he hangs out at your table, cracking his knuckles, waiting for you to reconsider the error of your ways.

"Frankie's watching it at home," says Mrs. Smiley, gesturing with her cell phone. "Says none of these kids will be half as funny as Jamie Grimm!"

The whole diner erupts with applause.

"Jay-mee! Jay-mee! Jay-mee!"

I soak it up for a few seconds because it feels great. But then I see Ray Romano come on the screen.

Oh, man. One of my all-time favorite stand-up comics and TV stars is the host of the semifinals. The TV audience is cheering for him the way I would. Hey, everybody loves Raymond.

"Thank you, thank you! Thank you so much! Oh, man, I'm not that good, I don't think. Let me just say, I can't tell you what a thrill it is to be hosting the Planet's Funniest Kid Comic semifinals!"

More applause.

"First I have to say hi to my kids at home. Hi, guys! Okay, go to bed! I have four kids. One daughter, three sons. And you know what? I don't care if you laugh or not. I'm just happy to be out of the house."

After a couple more jokes, Romano explains how we're going to see "sixteen incredible kid comics" tonight—the top two from the eight regional competitions. Next, he introduces the judges, who are—drumroll, please—Robin Williams, Ellen DeGeneres, and Chris Rock.

Wow. It's like my personal Mount Rushmore of stand-up comedy.

On the outside, I'm smiling. Inside? I'm weeping. I can't believe I came *this close* to meeting four of my comedy idols out in Las Vegas.

Gilda sees my lip quiver a little. It's hard to keep smiling when you feel like screaming.

"Next year," she whispers.

I nod.

Next year.

If there is a next year.

Chapter 57

I GUESS THIS IS THE END

Judy Nazemetz, the comedian who was nice to me in New York and Boston, kills big.

In comedy, killing is a good thing.

She slays the audience. Has them rolling in the aisles.

Ray Romano even comes up to her at the microphone after her set to personally congratulate her. Robin Williams gives her a standing ovation. Ellen DeGeneres is so thrilled, she's dancing. With Chris Rock.

Near the end of the hourlong show, Little Willy Creme comes on in what would've been my spot and basically bombs. Nobody in the TV audience or the diner laughs at any of his material. Not even Vincent O'Neil.

"Hey!" says Vincent. "He stole that doctor joke from me!"

When Little Willy is done (as in burnt toast), Ray Romano comes back onstage holding an envelope. He is ready to announce the "eight comedians moving on to Hollywood" for the finals.

But first, the offscreen announcer has to tell us how the kids heading out to Los Angeles will be the stars of a one-week reality TV show.

"Our Planet's Funniest Kid Comic camera crews will follow our nine finalists around Tinseltown as they prepare for the biggest performances of their young lives!"

"Wow," says Romano when he comes back onscreen. "You kids could become stars and make a ton of money. In my house, my wife gets all the money I make. I just get an apple and clean clothes every morning."

Everyone laughs.

Romano rips open the envelope and reads a list of eight names.

Judy Nazemetz is moving on to the finals. Little Willy is not.

Music starts. The announcer says something like "Join us in two weeks for..."

I aim the remote at the TV. Snap it off.

I don't want to hear any more about everything I could've had.

If I do, I might have to check myself into Uncle Frankie's old ICU room. Because my heart is breaking.

Can I tell you guys a big secret?

This is just between us, okay?

All I ever wanted was to be in the finals of the comedy contest. I didn't need to win. But I needed to show the world that no matter what life tossed at me, I'd figure out how to laugh my way through it.

I'd also like to maybe, someday, have a chance to walk again.

And I thought being on TV, maybe landing a talent agent and booking a couple of paying gigs, might give me a shot at the walking thing, too. Let's face it—operations and medical miracles cost money.

Well, anyway…

Zero out of two isn't so bad, right?

And I'm sorry my story has such a lousy ending.

Chapter 58

THE MIDDLE SCHOOL COMEDY CLUB

On the way to school Monday morning, Gilda Gold has an "amazingly awesome" idea.

"You should do your Vegas act here!"

"Um, Long Beach doesn't really have a comedy club...."

"So? You can do it at school. And since you missed your shot at performing on TV, I'll video the whole thing for posterity."

"Gilda, they're not going to just let us put on a show in the school auditorium. You have to ask for permission and fill out forms...."

"We don't need the auditorium!"

Gilda has that look in her eyes again. Her big blues look like two swirling whirlpools of excitement. She gets this way whenever she has one of her “amazingly awesome” ideas.

“We’ll stage it in the hallway. We can borrow that cordless microphone from the chorus room. Pierce can rig it up to an amplifier. That’s all you need, right?”

“Well, sometimes there’s a spotlight....”

“The drama club adviser is a pal. She’ll let us borrow it. We’re good to go.”

“Mrs. Kressin? Seriously?”

"Totally. You have your material ready to rock, right?"

"Pretty much," I say. "I was ninety percent locked down the day before Uncle Frankie had his heart attack."

"Well, you have all day to polish your routine. Showtime isn't until five minutes after the final bell."

When we reach the schoolyard, Stevie Kosgrov and his two hench-buddies, Zits and Useless, are waiting outside.

"What are you two geeks gabbing about?" he sneers.

Gilda props a hand on her hip and gets right in Stevie's face. "Jamie's doing his act. Today. Back hallway. Five minutes after the final bell."

Kosgrov narrows his eyes. Glares hard.

"Who's handling concessions and souvenirs?" he asks.

"Nobody. Not yet, anyway. You want in?"

"You bet. My profit margin on the whoopee cushions is phenomenal. Need to make a few calls. Maximize the merchandising..."

Yep. Not only has Stevie become a C-minus

student, it sounds like he's ready to run for president of Junior Achievement.

During homeroom, Gilda and Pierce do up a pretty cool flyer for the show.

By second period, I see it plastered all over the school. It's on every stall door in the bathrooms. There's one on every tray in the cafeteria. Gaynor's good with a roll of tape.

In the afternoon, Gilda and some of her friends turn the back corridor into a middle school replica of the Las Vegas strip, complete with blinking lights from the janitor, who dug a couple of strings from the school's holiday supply out of his closet.

When it's time for the afternoon announcements, the vice principal, Mr. Sour Patch himself, invites everyone to "join us after school for a command performance by the funniest kid on this or any other planet, our hometown hero, the one and only Jamie Grimm!"

When the final bell rings and school is over for the day, nobody races out the doors. They pack the back hallway, where Pierce and Gaynor have set up the cordless microphone and spotlight. Gilda is standing by to video the whole thing with her

TODAY
JAMIE
$
JAMIE FUNNY
JAMIE LIVE AT THE HALL
I'm gonna need a bigger broom.

smartphone. I can't believe the size of the crowd. Even the school bus drivers have come inside to catch my act.

This may be my biggest audience ever.

"Wow," says Vincent O'Neil when he sees the packed hallway. "It's every comedian's dream come true. Someday I hope I can perform for a crowd this size."

I smile. "How about doing it today?"

"What?"

"You can be my opening act."

"You're kidding!"

"Nope. Go on. And, Vincent?"

"Yeah?"

"Have fun."

He races off to grab the mic. And you know what? He's not half bad.

"Folks, coming up here I bumped into Stevie 'Knuckle Sandwich' Kosgrov, who, thank God, just told me that the last thing he wants to do is hurt me. But it *is* still on his to-do list."

Not bad at all.

Chapter 59

THE BEST AFTER-SCHOOL ACTIVITY EVER

Vincent does about five minutes of pretty funny stuff.

The crowd is all warmed up when it's time for me to go on.

"Yo, it's time for the main event," Gaynor shouts into the microphone when Vincent's set is done. "Ladies and gentlemen, the one and only Jaaaaaay-meeeeee Griiiiiiiiiiimm!"

I roll out to the center of the hall and grab the mic.

"Thank you," I say as the crowd cheers. "It's good to be in Long Beach. As my friend Joey Gaynor said, I am Jamie Grimm. Great name for a comedian,

right? *Grim*. Which, of course, means gloomy, grisly, and grumpy—put it all together and you end up with a group of very sad dwarves. Snow White would've had a real blast if she'd ended up in our hollow tree."

I move into some school-related material.

"Just finished cramming for my semester exams." I get a round of recognition applause. Everybody in the hallway was in the same boat.

"I am *sooooo* glad all that useless information is finally out of my brain. What happened in 1853? I don't know. Some guy fell off his horse. What? You think that's the wrong answer? I'm betting that somewhere in 1853, some dude slipped out of his saddle and ended up on his butt."

I do a little bit about the rhombus and the Invasion of the Trapezoids.

I tear up Madison Avenue and joke about advertising. "Have you seen this commercial for toilet paper? A bunch of bears who, you know… *go*…in the woods are hanging out in a bathroom, encouraging us to 'enjoy the go.' Seriously. That's the tagline. Enjoy the go. Since when did toilet paper become as much fun as a trip to Disney World? Wait. Don't answer that."

I tell the crowd what *I* enjoy: "Tearing down the open road in my uncle Frankie's Mustang convertible. There's nothing like it. Really. The wind whips through your hair, unless, you know, you're a gym teacher and all you have is head stubble.

"For me, it's like sticking my face under the hand dryer in a bathroom. My cheeks end up somewhere behind my ears. There are bugs in my teeth. More than usual. I have to floss constantly. And you can't really hear any music in a convertible, no matter how loud you crank up the tunes."

I explain that in my uncle Frankie's car, this can be a good thing.

"He listens to doo-wop music all the time. From the 1950s. What were people thinking back then? I mean, who writes lyrics like that?"

I recite a line from the Chords song like it's serious poetry:

"Sh-boom sh-boom.

Ya-da-da.

Da-da-da.

Da-da-da.

Da."

Then I toss up my hands.

"Am I missing something here?"

I make a crack about Warren G. Harding's middle name and Millard Fillmore saving us from French surfer dudes in Hawaii. "They'd call their baggy shorts 'baguettes.'" I discuss picking a girlfriend based on how easy it is to pronounce her name.

And then I move on to my big finish.

It's time to talk about the eight-hundred-pound gorilla sitting in the hallway.

My wheelchair.

Chapter 60

BRINGING DOWN THE SCHOOLHOUSE

I roll my chair forward a couple of inches.

"So the other day, this lady says to me, 'Excuse me, young man. What do you like to be called? Handicapped, disabled, or physically challenged?' And I said, 'How about Jamie?'"

The crowd chuckles. So I smile, to show it's okay. I know I am in a wheelchair and that my legs don't work.

"Now, as you guys can probably tell, when I'm in the Chair, I'm something of an outlaw."

The crowd laughs in disbelief.

"No, it's true. I break the law several times

every day. Usually on my way to and from school. Seriously. You know those blinking lights on every corner? I never, *ever* walk when they tell me to."

More laughs as I take off on a riff about the big red hand and the sideways-walking man.

"He looks like a guy escaping from a Lite Brite board. 'Sorry. Gotta go.' He just cocks his LED arms and hikes off. 'Enjoy the go, sir.' Man. He makes it look so easy. I wish I could do that."

I flex my hands so everybody can see my leather driving gloves.

"You're probably wondering why dudes in wheelchairs sometimes wear racing gloves. Is it to protect our sensitive hands from the rough tire treads and stench of rubber? Nah." I look from side to side like I'm about to reveal a deep, dark secret. "We do it because it looks so cool."

"It sure does!" shouts Cool Girl, who, of course, is in the hall.

I smile. Pretend to be super-cocky. "The rest of you guys? You'd look like total dorks if you walked around school all day wearing racing gloves. Me? I look *cool*."

I grip both handles, hard.

"Me and my wheelchair," I say like I'm a cheesy commercial announcer. "I'm in it for the parking."

The crowd cheers!

"I'm Jamie Grimm, and you guys have been a great audience! Thank you, Gilda! Thank you, Vincent! Thank you, Stevie, Pierce, Gaynor, and everybody else whose names I'm forgetting right now. Long Beach, I love you! You're better than Las Vegas! Now go see those trained Siberian tigers in the science lab!"

Nobody wants to leave.

Some want me to sign their whoopee cushions. (Stevie shoots me a thumbs-up; the merchandise is definitely moving.) Most just want to shake my

hand or pat me on the back or tell me what the funniest thing I said was.

Vincent O'Neil is one of the first in line to congratulate me.

"Thanks again for letting me go on, too!" he says. "Hey, you were funny."

“Maybe,” Vincent says, displaying yet another human emotion. This one looks like modesty. “But, Jamie? You were—and always will be—a bajillion times funnier!”

Gilda shoots me a wink and taps her smartphone. She recorded the whole thing.

Gaynor and Pierce are being congratulated, too. I guess for being my buds. Good. They deserve it.

Sitting in that corridor, soaking up the buzz and the love, I realize how lucky I am. To have so many good friends. To have had this chance to make them all laugh. To still have Uncle Frankie.

Hey, I really can’t afford to lose more family members anytime soon.

Did my spur-of-the-moment performance in the back corridor of Long Beach Middle School feel as good as it would have felt to perform on that stage at the Las Vegas Laugh Factory in front of Ray Romano, Robin Williams, Ellen DeGeneres, and Chris Rock?

Nah.

Not even close.

But still, it was very, very cool.

And I am one very, *very* lucky guy.

Chapter 61

ENCORE PERFORMANCE

I'm feeling so good, I don't want the day to ever end.

"You were hysterical," says Gaynor. "I wish my mom could've been here."

A lightbulb goes on over my head. I get an idea, too.

"Where is she?" I ask.

"Home. Probably in bed. She wasn't feeling so hot today."

"We should go pay her a visit. Do a repeat performance."

"We can't. I mean, *you* can't. Her immune system is still pretty wiped out from all the chemo. She's not supposed to see people for a few more days."

"Well, does she have a computer with Internet?"

"Yeah. A laptop."

I turn to Gilda. "How soon can you upload your video to YouTube?"

"How about now? Why?"

"Laughter is the best medicine, remember?"

Gilda smiles. "Give me like an hour. It's a big file."

Gilda and Pierce hurry off to the computer lab. Gaynor heads for home.

Me? Well, I just hope Mrs. Gaynor likes jokes about Millard Fillmore, doo-wop music, and bears pooping in a bathroom instead of the woods.

Because, as I learned the hard way, laughing can make you feel great even when you don't.

LIFE IS LIKE A YO-YO

After my Las-Vegas-in-Long-Beach performance, things are definitely looking up.

That Saturday, Uncle Frankie is back in the diner, twirling his yo-yo and telling people about the new items on the Good Eats by the Sea menu.

"Rabbit food," he says. "We've got a whole new section of healthy stuff. Lots of vegetables, fruits, and legumes."

"What are legumes?" I ask, because, face it, *legume* is a funny word.

"I have no idea, Jamie. But whatever they are, I gotta eat 'em instead of French fries."

Word spreads that Uncle Frankie is back and working the grill again. Before long, the diner is

NEW! RABBIT FOOD MENU
F
F

packed. It's like Long Beach is giving their hero an indoor ticker-tape parade, only instead of tossing up confetti, people are blowing the paper wrappers off their straws to make party streamers.

All the old customers are back, including Mr. Burdzecki.

"Is very good to see you look so healthy, my friend," he says.

"Thanks, Boris," says Uncle Frankie.

"Your heart attack, it reminds me of a joke. Pay close attention, Jamie."

"Yes, sir."

"A man, we will call him Fred, came home from his Sunday round of golf later than normal and looked very tired. 'Bad day at the course?' his wife asked.

"'Everything was going fine,' said Fred. 'Then Harry had a heart attack and died on the tenth tee.' 'Oh, that's awful!' said the wife. 'You are not kidding,' said Fred. 'For the whole back nine, it was hit the ball, drag Harry, hit the ball, drag Harry.'"

Uncle Frankie cracks up. "Good one, Boris."

Mr. Burdzecki wags his finger at Uncle Frankie. "Eat your leafy greens. I do not wish to drag you up and down and all over town like Fred drags Harry."

"Aye, aye," says Uncle Frankie.

One by one, everybody squeezes up to the counter to shake Uncle Frankie's hand, say something funny, and wish him well. Some even bring yo-yos.

"We figure you need the exercise!" says a lady who gives Frankie a bright-yellow smiley-face yo-yo that flashes LEDs as it spins.

"Hey, you could start a new aerobics craze," cracks another. "The yo-yo workout!"

"No," jokes somebody else. "The yo-yo diet. You have to twirl all your food on a string before you can eat it."

Just about all the customers get in on the act and give their best shot at a yo-yo joke.

"Why did the yo-yo cross the road? Because it was walking the dog!"

"What did one yo-yo say to the other yo-yo when he saw him? Yo!"

Oh, boy, this is getting painful! But Uncle Frankie loves it. "One thing I like about yo-yos," he says, "is that for every down, there's an up. Thanks, everyone!"

I try to cut off the yo-yo jokes with a quick Kevin James quip. "Well, working out with his yo-yo might help Uncle Frankie lower his cholesterol. But Kevin James, who's so big he sweats when he peels an orange, has different fitness goals. He says he wants to lose enough weight that his stomach doesn't jiggle when he brushes his teeth."

Everyone cracks up. I topped them all.

And then Uncle Frankie tops me.

"You know, Jamie, the older you get, the tougher it is to lose weight, because by then, your body and your fat are really good friends."

Uncle Frankie knows a thing or two about good friends. He's got a ton.

And I don't think he's going to lose any of 'em anytime soon.

Chapter 63

KNOCK, KNOCK! WHO'S THERE?

By Monday, things are pretty much back to normal.

I'm in my garage room at the Smileys' after school, doing my homework. I haven't cracked open my comedy notebooks or jotted down any new ideas for fresh routines since that fateful day when Aunt Smiley and I called the people out in Hollywood to let them know I wouldn't be able to appear in Las Vegas.

I mean, what's the point?

Unless Gilda organizes another hallway performance, I won't really need new jokes anytime soon.

It's okay. I'm cool with it.

Not having to worry about my comedy act gives

me more time to concentrate on my schoolwork—what Uncle Frankie called my meat and potatoes. Now that he's on his heart-healthy diet, he'd probably call it my baked chicken and wild rice.

Except for severely missing his burgers, fries, and milk shakes, Uncle Frankie is doing great. The diner has never been busier, and he's never seemed happier.

Gaynor tells me his mom has watched my YouTube act "at least a dozen times" and tells him to "enjoy the go" every morning when he heads out the door for school. Mrs. Gaynor is between treatments. Everything is going great, and her doctors are really optimistic.

So, yeah—normal is okay. It's not as glitzy as Las Vegas, but it's good.

Then there's this knock on my garage door.

A very loud banging.

Now what?

I say a quick prayer: *Please don't let it be Stevie Kosgrov*. He didn't sell every one of his whoopee cushions at my hallway show, and the people who make them in China don't believe in refunds.

"Jamie?" It's Mrs. Smiley.

"Open this door!" Mr. Smiley.

Uh-oh. This could be urgent.

I reach over and undo the lock. Yank it open.

"What's up?" I say. "Is everybody okay?"

"You tell us," says Mr. Smiley.

That's when Mrs. Smiley hands me an envelope.

Chapter 64

HOW FEDEX CHANGED MY LIFE—FAST!

"FedEx just delivered this for you," says Aunt Smiley.

"We've never had a FedEx truck come to our house before," adds my uncle.

Aunt Smiley hands me the envelope. It's from Joe Amodio, executive producer of the Planet's Funniest Kid Comic Contest, Hollywood, California.

"It's probably just a certificate or something," I say, the envelope trembling in my hands. "I bet they send one to all the participants."

"Jamie?" says Uncle Smiley.

"Yes, sir?"

"Nobody sends certificates of participation in an overnight FedEx envelope. That's what the regular mail is for!"

"Open it, hon," urges Aunt Smiley.

So I do.

Very, very slowly. It's like I can't get my fingers to work.

"Pull that tab thingy," coaches Uncle Smiley, who's as eager as I am to see what's inside the first FedEx envelope to ever arrive at the Smiley residence.

I tug the tear strip off the back. Pry open the cardboard envelope.

There's a letter tucked inside.

"What's it say?" asks Aunt Smiley, who has her eyes closed and her fingers crossed.

I slide the sheet of paper out of the envelope. (Heart transplants probably take less time.)

Drumroll, please...

"It's from the executive producer of the comedy contest," I report.

"And?" says Mr. Smiley, giving me double hurry-up-already hand rolls.

I swallow hard and read the letter out loud:

"'Dear Jamie: As you know, at the semifinals in Las Vegas, eight contestants were selected to move on to the final round of the Planet's Funniest Kid Comic Contest in Hollywood. This Saturday, we're taping our Judges' Picks Wild Card Show to find our final finalist. After checking out the YouTube video of your recent performance at school, the judges and I would like to invite you to be one of our wild card contestants. One of you, the winner of this Saturday's competition, will go on to join our other eight finalists in Hollywood.'"

"What does that mean?" asks Uncle Smiley.

"They saw the video we put online for Joey's mom," I say. "Seems there's another round of semifinals...."

Aunt Smiley has an "aha!" look on her face.

"So that's why the TV announcer said the reality show camera crews would be following 'nine finalists around Tinseltown' when only eight comics were picked to go to Hollywood on TV. I thought he was just bad with math, like Stevie."

"And," says Uncle Smiley, having his own "aha" moment, "that show they were just about to tell us to watch in two weeks when Jamie snapped off the TV..." He quickly counts to fourteen on his fingers. "That's *this* show! This Saturday is two weeks from that Saturday!"

I can't believe this is happening. I don't have to wait till next year. My second chance at the comedy contest is only six days away.

I read the rest of the letter. Fast.

"Okay. The show tapes at two o'clock. This

Saturday afternoon. Goes on air at eight that night. They say we're supposed to call the production office ASAP to arrange air travel and hotel accommodations for me and 'my family.' "

"Woo-hoo!" says Mr. Smiley. "We're your family!"

"Where's this show being taped?" asks Mrs. Smiley.

"Uh, let's see. Las Vegas. The Laugh Factory! Just like the first semifinals!"

My aunt leans down and gives me a humongous hug. "I'm so happy for you, Jamie. I prayed and prayed that someday you'd have another chance to make your dreams come true."

"I'm happy, too," says Uncle Smiley. "I've always wanted to visit Las Vegas."

“We’ll take the whole family,” says Aunt Smiley. “Make it a mini-vacation.”

“I guess we should call the production office,” I say. “Let them know we’re coming.”

“Here,” says Uncle Smiley, handing me his cell phone. “Call! Hurry!”

“Can I call someone else first?” I ask.

“What? Who?”

“My friend Gilda Gold. If it weren’t for her, none of this would’ve happened.”

“Call her!” says Aunt Smiley.

I do.

When I tell Gilda the good news, she screams so loudly I’m guessing you can probably hear her at your house.

Chapter 65

FLYING HIGH (WITH OR WITHOUT AN AIRPLANE)

Thursday afternoon, me and all the Smileys (except Ol' Smiler, who's bunking with Uncle Frankie in my old room) board an airplane headed for Las Vegas.

Of course, I have to board first with the "anyone needing special assistance or a little more time getting down the Jetway" crowd.

Just another perk of life in the Chair.

Uncle Frankie threw me a big bon voyage party at the diner Wednesday night. Gilda—my favorite moviemaker in the entire universe—was there. So were Gaynor (who brought his mom), Pierce, Cool Girl, and half of Long Beach Middle School—including a lot of teachers and Mr. Sour Patch.

I made a little speech.

First I thanked my friends and everybody at school for "giving me so much great material to work with."

Then I thanked Gilda for coming up with the whole idea of me doing my Vegas act at school and for posting my performance on the Web.

And finally, I thanked the man who was the first person to ever tell me that I had talent and then did everything he could to help me nurture it while also teaching me how to flip burgers and yo-yo at the same time.

Uncle Frankie.

"I just wish you could come with us," I told him while we were passing around slices of the Good Luck, Jamie cake he wouldn't be able to eat.

Uncle Frankie shrugged. "Doc says it's too early for me to fly. Or get all worked up watching you compete onstage. But here. Put this in your pocket."

He hands me a dinged-up old plastic yo-yo.

"That's the Duncan Jeweled I twirled when I won

the Brooklyn championship. Maybe it'll bring you luck, too."

That yo-yo is in my pocket on the plane. It'll be in my pocket the whole time I'm in Vegas.

For me, this Judges' Picks Wild Card Show is like the Super Bowl, *American Idol*, *The Voice*, *America's Got Talent*, and *Dancing with the Stars* all wrapped up into one.

Well, maybe not *Dancing with the Stars*.

The people producing the Planet's Funniest Kid Comic Contest bought us all first-class tickets. That means the flight attendants keep coming around to ask if we need or want anything.

"No, thanks!" I say, because I'm too excited to nibble the free goodies they keep passing out.

What's happening is unbelievable.

I'm flying to Las Vegas.

To do a comedy act.

In front of judges who happen to be some of my all-time favorite comedians.

I feel like I'm sailing over the moon as we fly across the country. It's enough to make me dizzy. I might even need to grab that airsickness bag.

Stevie Kosgrov, on the other hand, is, well, still Stevie Kosgrov.

He eats every free snack the flight attendants offer. He has two lunches. He's even hoarding tiny packs of peanuts in his carry-on bag.

As the FASTEN SEAT BELT lights come on and we make our initial descent into the Las Vegas area, Stevie turns to me.

"I only have one question, Crip. Do they give out like a ninth runner-up award to the dude who comes in last? 'Cause I'm making room for it on the mantel at home."

Yup.

Leave it to Stevie to remind me that every time I enter one of these contests, I have a better chance of coming out a loser than actually winning it.

Chapter 66

LAS VEGAS OR "LOST WAGES"?

Thursday afternoon and most of Friday, we have free time.

"Just be at the Laugh Factory by one o'clock Saturday," says one of the production assistants in charge of coordinating talent for the show. "Until then, enjoy. Have a ball. Go out and do Las Vegas!"

Much to my dismay, Mr. and Mrs. Smiley not only want to see every inch of the fabled Las Vegas Strip, they want to take pictures of it, too.

Can I just mention how crowded the sidewalks are on Las Vegas Boulevard—twenty-four hours a day?

I spend a lot of time looking at sequined butts. And weaving my way through pretty wobbly foot traffic. And not looking at all the stuff Aunt Smiley tells me not to look at because it's "for adults only."

But we also have fun posing for snapshots with lots of Elvis, Batman, Teenage Mutant Ninja Turtle, and Angry Bird impersonators.

We gawk at all the dazzling light shows and wild architecture. I'm blown away by the gigantic marquees announcing the comics doing shows while we're in town: David Spade, Jay Leno, Kathy Griffin, Tim Allen, Wayne Brady...even Bill Cosby is here! There are also funny magicians (Penn & Teller) and a guy who does comedy hypnosis!

Also, you wouldn't believe all the incredible casino buildings up and down the Strip. One looks like a pyramid. Another is a miniature New York City, complete with its own Statue of Liberty and Brooklyn Bridge (not to mention an awesome roller coaster). It's right across the street from a hotel that looks like a castle. A little farther up the road, you'll find Paris (just look for the Eiffel Tower) and Venice (which has actual air-conditioned canals inside).

I know I'll be onstage soon, but there's still time to cook up new material for my act, and Vegas is a

WELCOME
TO Fabulous
LAS VEGAS
NEVADA
DRIVE-THRU
WEDDING CHAPEL
24 HRS 7 DAYS
DRIVE-THRU
DIVORC
They say, "What Happens in Vegas Stays in Vegas." Just like your money.
WILD CARD FOR TH WIN

LIVE
COMEDY
EVERY
NIG
m
m&m
THEE AMAZING
ELVII
Steve-a
Las Vegas
20 TOP
PLACES
TO
BORE
THE

comic gold mine. It's funnier than New York City and the J. Walter Thompson advertising agency combined.

Watching the Smileys tour the city is another gold mine. They're hilarious, too.

For instance, even though kids aren't allowed on the gambling floors of the casinos (babies and blackjack don't mix), I get to watch Mr. Smiley lose a ton of money in slot machines, which are everywhere. The airport. The hotel lobby. The burger joints. The handicapped stall in the men's room.

Okay. I made that last one up.

I think Uncle Smiley likes the blinking lights and noises. He never wins, but he hears a lot of cool *whoop-whoop* and *bing-bing* sound effects.

He also likes the showgirls, who look like they're wearing flamingos or maybe pink potted ferns on top of their heads.

Mrs. Smiley likes the guys in Roman costumes at Caesars Palace—including some statues that come to life to heckle each other.

And did I mention the pirate ship battle outside the Treasure Island casino? Hilarious.

Stevie? His favorite stop is M&M's World, where the walls are lined with clear plastic bins filled with every color M&M imaginable. Stevie doesn't use a plastic bag to load up. He just positions his mouth near the chutes at the bottom of the silos and opens wide.

Yes, Las Vegas is hysterical. Unbelievably funny.

I just hope people here say the same thing about me when I roll offstage.

Tomorrow!

Chapter 67

THE FEAR FACTORY

It's Saturday, 1:45 PM.

Fifteen minutes till the show starts.

I'm backstage at the Laugh Factory. In the shadows, I can see seven other very nervous young comedians. Pacing. Muttering jokes. On the stage, TV technicians are scurrying around with cameras and cables and extremely bright lights.

I see the single microphone stand at center stage, right in front of the glowing Laugh Factory logo.

I now know exactly where and when I will die.

Where: onstage.

When: the minute they call my name, which I can't really remember. Because I'm like that forest out in Arizona: totally petrified!

(Yes, "identify six national parks" was one of the questions on my recent geography exam.)

My knees twitch in an involuntary spasm that makes my shoes chatter against my wheelchair footplates. It sounds like I'm tap-dancing.

Nervous much?

You bet.

I'm so afraid that I'm going to freak out and freeze. That I'll just roll onstage and drool for three minutes. That I am going to, once again, CHOKE. This time on national TV.

The only good news? This isn't a *live* broadcast like *SNL*. The show won't be on until eight o'clock. There will be plenty of time to edit me out completely. (Maybe they can put up a title card explaining that my appearance has been canceled due to technical difficulties—because my brain short-circuited.)

And then, to make things worse, Ray Romano ambles over to shake my hand.

"Hey, Jamie," he says. "Caught your act on YouTube. Funny stuff."

And what do I say to my comic idol in reply?

"Uh, er, um—ba-doh, ba-doo, ba-doodle-ay."

Yes, if this were 1957, I could write doo-wop lyrics.

A stage manager shouts, "Five minutes, everybody! Five minutes!"

I'm sweating like a pig in a bacon factory. A turkey on Thanksgiving Eve.

Suddenly, somebody is shaking me.

Stevie Kosgrov is backstage. He's jerking me back and forth in my chair. Bouncing me up and down on my cushioned seat.

"Don't you dare black out, freak out, choke, or whatever it is you do when you go all spastic before one of these comedy contests. This one is gonna be on TV. *Tee-Vee!* And I will be in the audience, which will also be on TV. This will be the biggest, most awesome night of my life, so don't you blow it. Or I swear I'll put your face in a wheelchair, too!"

Strangely, that helps.

I snap out of it.

I remember my name. Jamie Grimm.

Now all I have to do is remember a few of my jokes.

Chapter 68

THE WILD WILD-CARD CONTESTANTS

"Welcome back to the search for the Planet's Funniest Kid Comic!" booms an offscreen announcer. "Tonight—it's the Judges' Picks Wild Card Show."

It's supposed to be an hour-long program, so each comedian is only given three minutes at the microphone. That means twenty-four minutes for jokes, maybe twenty minutes for commercials, and sixteen for Ray Romano, Chris Rock, Ellen DeGeneres, and our "surprise celebrity guest judge," Jerry Seinfeld, to crack wise.

I'm supposed to go on last. The eighth comic up.

This gives me a little more time to mop the tsunami of sweat off my face. Fortunately, Mrs. Smiley grabbed a towel out of the hotel gym for me. Too bad she didn't find a sponge or a squeegee.

Ray Romano starts the show talking about his own kids and how he'll do anything to get out of the house these days. "Does anybody need anything? Anything at all? Anything from the, uh, motor vehicle bureau, how about that? Can I register something for you?"

The crowd laughs and claps.

I am only vaguely aware of the other contestants.

There's an African-American kid who break-dances while delivering material that rivals Chris Rock's best routines. In fact, some of his material comes directly *from* Chris Rock's routines: "My mother is the kind of woman you don't want to be in line behind at the supermarket. She has coupons for coupons."

I guess the kid is more of a dancer than a joke writer.

There's also a gangly seven-foot-tall guy from New Orleans. His name is Hurricane and he's kind of intimidating. He has an accent like an alligator as he talks about life in Louisiana. "Possums sleep in the middle of the road with their feet up. People actually eat okra. *Fixinto* is one word. And it's a verb. *I'm fixinto go to the store*."

Clara Rodriguez from Miami does all her jokes in two languages. Spanish, then English.

"Entra un tipo muy feo con un loro en un bar, y el camarero pregunta: -¿Habla el animal? -¡Y yo qué sé!, responde el loro."

Jerry Seinfeld chuckles. Guess he speaks Spanish.

Clara does the same joke again. "An ugly guy walks into a bar with a parrot. The bartender asks, 'Does the animal speak?' 'I don't know,' replies the parrot."

The bilingual trick is kind of cool. And educational. It's also *extremely* slow. Three jokes and her three minutes is up.

As the other contestants take the stage one by one, my brain shifts into Mission Control mode. *"Ten...nine...eight..."*

I'm counting down to blastoff. The moment when Ray Romano calls my name and I roll out onstage to explode with a fiery burst of high-octane comedy.

Or choke.

One of those.

Like Chris Rock says, what do you mean "Red meat will kill you?" Don't eat red meat? No, don't eat green meat!
What do you call a lazy crawfish? A slobster!
Who Dat ARMY
Doctor: ¿Qué es lo que le ha traído por aquí? Paciente: Una ambulancia, ¿por qué?*
*A doctor says, "What brought you here?" The patient answers, "An ambulance. Why?"

Chapter 69

WHO AM I? WHERE AM I?

Comedian number seven, a kid from Milwaukee who's wearing a cheesehead hat, takes his bow.

"Okay," says Ray Romano. "That was, uh, very *gouda*, I guess. Next up, our final wild card contestant…hailing from my corner of the country, New York—let's welcome to the stage…Jamie Grimm!"

I head out onto the stage and…

And this is why you shouldn't read, people! You're TOTAL suckers! You paid like, what? Thirty-three and a third cents for two TOTALLY EMPTY pages. Hey, I don't know if that number's right. You do the math (and my history homework, too, OR ELSE). Or, maybe you went to "the library," wherever that is. But even if the book was free, come on—your time's gotta be worth something, right? Eh, maybe not. Anyway, I mean, big surprise. Right before he goes on, Jamie chokes—AGAIN!!!

Chapter 70

AND THE WINNER IS???

Sorry about that.

Didn't mean to totally abandon ship.

But to tell you the truth, I don't remember anything about what happened while I was onstage. All I remember is Ray Romano calling my name, and me rolling my chair into the bright circle of light behind the microphone stand and slipping into a total mental fog.

Did the audience laugh?

I don't know. I can't remember.

Did I win? I don't know.

Yes, you're right, I would've remembered winning, no matter how deeply I disappeared into that weirdly blank blackout zone.

But the winner won't be announced until tonight, when the show's on TV. I guess the judges want to play back the performances. See how we look on camera, not just in person at the comedy club.

So I'll find out if I won at the same moment the rest of America hears about it.

★ ★ ★

I'm with the Smileys in our hotel suite at the Tropicana.

The seven other contestants and their families are on the same floor, in their own suites. There's a crew with a portable video camera out in the hall, just waiting for their cue to barge through a door and zoom in on whoever wins when Ray Romano reads the results.

So, for better or worse, I get to watch the whole show.

"Good luck, Jamie!" says Mrs. Smiley from the couch when the show's opening music blares out of the plasma screen TV.

I hear gagging.

Stevie is behind the couch, where his parents can't see him, pretending to strangle himself. I guess he knows I choked. Hey, he was out in the audience during my three minutes. I was stumbling blindly in that mental blizzard.

We watch Hurricane and the break-dancer. The bilingual girl and an Elvis Presley impersonator, who says, "Uh, thank you, thank you very much" every time anybody laughs or applauds. It's about half his act.

A stubby kid in a baggy suit and loose tie comes out to do a junior Rodney Dangerfield routine. His catchphrase is "I tell ya, folks—it's tough being a kid," and he is hysterical. I crack up when he talks about his mother licking wads of Kleenex that have been in her purse "since the Nixon administration" to wipe a peanut butter smudge off his face. "In the cafeteria. At school. I tell ya, folks—it's tough being a kid."

Finally, Cheesehead comes on. But I don't hear a word he says because I know I'll be the next comic behind the microphone.

On national TV!

I have never been so nervous. It's like I'm in the audience for my own show—or the pews for my own funeral. I feel the way parents must feel when they go to school band concerts and their kid has a solo on the oboe or the clarinet. One of the squeakier instruments.

"Don't blow it, son. Please, don't blow it."

I'm thinking the same thing.

And suddenly, there I am. In my wheelchair. In the spotlight. Smiling.

And BOOM!

I launch into three minutes of my best material *ever*.

It's my life.

What it's like in the Chair. My friends at school. Watching TV commercials. Slot machines in the handicapped stalls.

It's everything I've observed or imagined. Only funnier.

You know what? I think I nailed it. I really do.

Win or lose, at least I know I gave it my all.

Was my killer performance good enough to win? Was I better than little Rodney Dangerfield, who was absolutely incredible?

We still don't know.

Ray Romano pulls a Ryan Seacrest and says the winner is…going to be announced…right after the break.

And so we watch a commercial.

It's those dumb bears with their toilet paper again.

Finally, at long last, Ray Romano is about to rip open the envelope telling us who is moving on to the finals in Hollywood.

But before he can, our hotel door flies open.

Three guys toting a TV camera, a boom microphone, and a very bright spotlight race across the room and surround me so they can jab their gear in my face.

Yep.

I won!

Chapter 71

HOMECOMING KING

I've never been to Hollywood (well, not yet, anyway), but my welcome home was bigger and better than any red-carpet movie premiere.

It feels like everybody is here, including folks I'm pretty sure aren't, like the president of the United States and the Black Eyed Peas.

After I shake a bajillion hands and eat a ton of cake, Cool Girl comes running up to my chair to give me a big hug.

Two seconds after she lets go, Gilda Gold pushes her way through the crowd and gives me an even bigger hug.

"I knew you could do it, Jamie!" she says. "You funny!"

I smile. But I see the look in her eye.

We need to talk.

NEWS LIVE
Who is he?
I think he won the Wheelchair Olympics...
Jamie
J.G.!
Jamie! Is it true you'll be representing Earth in the Galaxy's Funniest Kid Comic Contest?
Jamie! Who are you wearing?
JAMIE FUNNIE
Do we get the day off for this?
My face has been so sore, I've been thinking of putting an ice pack on it.
I told him, he funny!
It's hard to get used to all this smiling!

This is your pilot speaking... can one of the Secret Service guys get me Jamie Grimm's autograph?
JAMIE FUNNIE
J.G.!
GRIMM IS GOLD
JAMIE
GRIMM FOR THE WIN
Agent Alpha to Agent Beta... do you think POTUS will let us get our picture taken with Jamie Grimm? Over...
Copy that! I hope so. That kid is the funniest! Over and out.
Mr. Grimm, I had to leave Washington to shake your hand.
O.M.G.! OBAMA!
Of course you did—because his hand is here in Long Island!

Chapter 12

GIRL FRIEND OR GIRLFRIEND?

Gilda and I sneak away from the crowd and head down to the boardwalk.

"First off," I say, "I really need to thank you. If it weren't for you, I don't think any of this would've happened."

Gilda shrugs, which makes the curly hair under her BoSox baseball cap bob and bounce.

"I just did what any good friend would do."

"That's just it," I say. "I want us to always be friends, Gilda. Good friends."

"Relax, Jamie," Gilda says with a laugh—the same incredibly unique laugh I can always hear, no matter how many other laughs are bubbling up around it. "We'll always be good, good friends. The best."

"Awesome," I say, breathing a sigh of relief. "Because I think hugging and kissing and junk can *totally* ruin a friendship."

"Yep," says Gilda. "It sure can."

And then she kisses me.

On the lips.

It's very soft and very sweet—with a hint of strawberry.

I kind of like it.

Was it better than my first kiss with Cool Girl?

Not totally sure. Check back with me on that.

This whole friends-who-are-more-than-friends dealio is confusing. I need to think it over.

So I kiss Gilda back.

Just to make sure I've done enough research for all that thinking I need to do.

Chapter 73

IF I HAD $110,000...

Oh, in case I forgot to mention it—which I probably did, because I've been kind of busy being excited about winning and confused about girls—when I won the wild card contest out in Las Vegas, I also won a trophy and a check for ten thousand dollars.

It was one of those jumbo, Publishers Clearing House–sized cardboard checks. Very hard to stow in the overhead bins on the airplane trip home. Definitely wouldn't fit in my wallet. I had to sign it on the back with a paintbrush.

Uncle Frankie says the money needs to go into a savings account to help pay for my college education.

The Smileys agree.

Well, all of them except Stevie, who instantly sees me as his biggest shakedown target ever. If he can force me into forking over my ten-thousand-dollar prize, it will set some kind of new middle school indoor bullying record.

Sorry, Stevie.

For now, the money is safely deposited in my brand-new bank account, where it will wait, hoping to be joined by the hundred thousand dollars the first-place winner of the Planet's Funniest Kid Comic competition will take home from Hollywood.

That's right. If I can win one more stand-up comedy contest (without ever standing up), I will have one hundred and ten thousand dollars in the bank.

That might be enough money to pay for the experimental surgery that could help me walk again.

Or it could pay for college.

Or I could buy the world's first hover wheelchair. With a jet pack of booster rockets strapped on the back so I could float above the crowded sidewalks and zip my way through traffic.

VEGAS
WED
THU
FRI

Wait a second. Forget high-tech, space-age wheelchairs. With a hundred and ten thousand dollars, maybe I could hire the front line of the Green Bay Packers to carry me wherever I wanted to go.

Or I could just buy everybody at Uncle Frankie's diner (except, of course, Uncle Frankie) a year's supply of chocolate milk shakes and French fries.

Okay. This is good. I need to jot this stuff down in a notebook. Could be a new bit for Hollywood.

Which is only a month away!

Epilogue

COMING SOON: JAMIE'S HOLLYWOOD BLOCKBUSTER!

Okay, here it is: my very own "coming attractions" trailer for what happens next!

Cue the cool movie soundtrack music.

I fly out to Hollywood and meet all sorts of movie stars, including C-3PO and R2-D2, who fall into a swimming pool and rust.

Instead of handprints in wet cement outside TCL Chinese Theatre on Hollywood Boulevard, I do tire treads.

Uncle Frankie comes with me and is immediately cast as the male lead in the kung fu action flick *Yo-Yo-Pow!* He uses his yo-yos like nunchakus.

I think I see my cousin over there....

I studied the flying-crane yo-yo form for decades!
I thought you were faster than a speeding bullet. I've been waiting to change for ages.
TELEPHONE

Stevie Kosgrov finds work as a Hollywood stunt man. He's very good at knocking things over or blowing them up.

Reality TV show cameras follow me and the other finalists all over Hollywood. They catch me riding the sweet waves in the warm Pacific.

Friendly comic Judy is now my main rival for the crown.

Do we kiss? What about Gilda and Cool Girl? Do I spend all my prize money on ChapStick and breath mints?

Beavis and Butt-Head become my close personal friends, even though, you know, they're cartoons. Hey, it's Hollywood. If you can dream it, it can happen! Or they can at least fake it.

★ ★ ★

Postscripterino: I don't know if any of this stuff will actually happen.

I'm not exactly a psychic. I'm just a kid trying to be funny and enjoy this wild and crazy ride.

I find it helps if you never take anything, including yourself, too seriously.

I'm Jamie Grimm. And you guys have been a great audience! See you in Hollywood!

I'll wash, you dry.
Works for me.

P.S. FROM JAMIE

If you like making people laugh as much as I do, you know you need a whole lot of funny jokes and one-liners. The Web is full of sites that'll help you build your own comedy routine. Maybe you and a friend can even act out Abbott and Costello's classic "Who's on First?" skit. You can find the full script here: psu.edu/dept/inart10_110/inart10/whos.html

For other jokes, you might want to check out some of my favorite websites:

ahajokes.com/kids_jokes.html
jokesbykids.com
greatcleanjokes.com/jokes/kids-jokes
ducksters.com/jokes
rd.com/jokes/kids
101kidz.com/jokes

HIGH ADVENTURE ON THE HIGH SEAS!

Turn the page for a sneak peek at James Patterson's exciting series.

AVAILABLE NOW

1

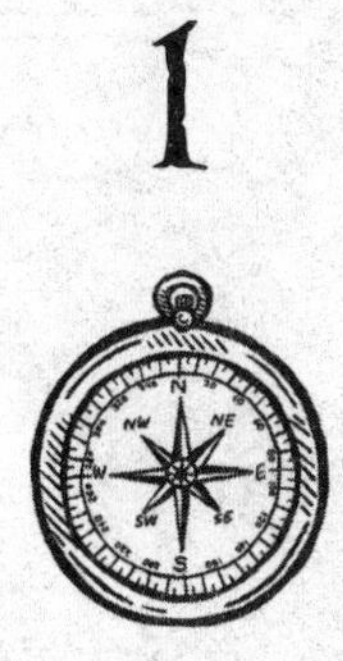

Let me tell you about the last time I saw my dad.

We were up on deck, rigging our ship to ride out what looked like a perfect storm.

Well, it was perfect if you were the storm. Not so much if you were the people being tossed around the deck like wet gym socks in a washing machine.

We had just finished taking down and tying off the sails so we could run on bare poles.

"Lash off the wheel!" my dad barked to my big brother, Tailspin Tommy. "Steer her leeward and lock it down!"

A PERFECT STORM!
The LOST
A NOT-So-Perfect Twin Brother

"On it!"

Tommy yanked the wheel hard and pointed our bow downwind. He looped a bungee cord through the wheel's wooden spokes to keep us headed in that direction.

"Now get below, boys. Batten down the hatches. Help your sisters man the pumps."

Tommy grabbed hold of whatever he could to steady himself and made his way down into the deckhouse cabin.

Just then, a monster wave lurched over the starboard side of the ship and swept me off my feet. I slid across the slick deck like a hockey puck on ice. I might've gone overboard if my dad hadn't reached down and grabbed me a half second before I became shark bait.

"Time to head downstairs, Bick!" my dad shouted in the raging storm as rain slashed across his face.

"No!" I shouted back. "I want to stay up here and help you."

"You can help me more by staying alive and not

letting *The Lost* go under. Now hurry! Get below."

"B-b-but—"

"Go!"

He gave me a gentle shove to propel me up the tilting deck. When I reached the deckhouse, I grabbed onto a handhold and swung myself around and through the door. Tommy had already headed down to the engine room to help with the bilge pumps.

Suddenly, a giant sledgehammer of salt water slammed into our starboard side and sent the ship tipping wildly to the left. I heard wood creaking. We tilted over so far I fell against the wall while our port side slapped the churning sea.

We were going to capsize. I could tell.

But *The Lost* righted itself instead, the ship tossing and bucking like a very angry beached whale.

I found the floor and shoved the deckhouse hatch shut. I had to press my body up against it. Waves kept pounding against the door. The water definitely wanted me to let it in.

That wasn't going to happen. Not on my watch.

I cranked the door's latch to bolt it tight.

I would, of course, reopen the door the instant my dad finished doing whatever else needed to be done up on deck and made his way aft to the cabin. But, for now, I had to stop *The Lost* from taking on any more water.

If that was even possible.

The sea kept churning. *The Lost* kept lurching. The storm kept sloshing seawater through every crack and crevice it could find.

Me? I started panicking. Because I had a sinking feeling (as in "We're gonna sink!") that this could be the end.

I was about to be drowned at sea.

Is twelve years old too young to die?

Apparently, the Caribbean Sea didn't think so.

I waited and waited, but my dad never made it aft to the deckhouse cabin door.

Through the forward windows, I could see waves crashing across our bobbing bow. I could see the sky growing even darker. I could see a life preserver rip free from its rope and fly off the ship like a doughnut-shaped Frisbee.

But I couldn't see Dad.

I suddenly realized that my socks were soaked with the seawater that was slopping across the floor. And I was up on the main deck.

"Beck?" I cried out. "Tommy? Storm?"

My sisters and brother were all down in the lower cabins and equipment rooms, where the water was undoubtedly deeper.

They were trapped down there!

I dashed down the four steep steps into the hull quarters as quickly as I could. The water was up to my ankles, then my knees, then my thighs,

and, finally, my waist. You ever try to run across the shallow end of a swimming pool? That's what I was up against. But I had to find my family.

Well, what was left of it.

I trudged from door to door, frantically searching for my siblings.

They weren't in the engine room, the galley,

or my parents' cabin. I knew they couldn't be in The Room, because its solid steel door was locked tight and it was totally off-limits to all of us.

I slogged my way forward as the ship kept rocking and rolling from side to side. Whatever wasn't nailed down was thumping around inside the cupboards and cabinets. I heard cans of food banging into plastic dishes that were knocking over clinking coffee mugs.

I started pounding on the walls in the narrow corridor with both fists. The water was up to my chest.

"Hey, you guys? Tommy, Beck, Storm! Where are you?"

No answer.

Of course my brother and sisters probably couldn't hear me, because the tropical storm outside was screaming even louder than I was.

Suddenly, up ahead, a door burst open.

Tommy, who was seventeen and had the kind of bulging muscles you only get from crewing on a sailing ship your whole life, had just put his shoulder to the wood to bash it open.

"Where's Dad?" he shouted.

"I don't know!" I shouted back.

That's when Beck and my big sister, Storm, trudged out of the cabin that was now their water-logged bedroom. A pair of 3-D glasses was floating on the surface of the water. Beck plucked them up and put them on. She'd been wearing them ever since our mom disappeared.

"Was Dad on a safety line?" asked Storm, sounding as scared and worried as I felt.

All I could do was shake my head.

Beck looked at me, and even though her 3-D glasses were shading her eyes, I could tell she was thinking the same thing I was. We're twins. It happens.

In our hearts, we both knew that Dad was gone.

Because anything up on deck that hadn't been tied down had been washed overboard by now.

From the sad expressions on their faces, I knew Storm and Tommy had figured it out, too. Maybe they'd been looking out a porthole when that life preserver went flying by.

Shivering slightly, we all moved together to form a close circle and hug each other tight.

The four of us were the only family we had left.

Tommy, who'd been living on boats longer than any of us, started mumbling an old sailor's prayer:

"Though Death waits off the bow, we'll not answer to him now."

I hoped he was right.

But I had a funny feeling that Death might not take no for an answer.